THE WIDOW'S GUIDE TO EDIBLE MUSHROOMS

THE WIDOW'S GUIDE TO EDIBLE MUSHROOMS

Chauna Craig

Press 53
Winston-Salem

Press 53, LLC
PO Box 30314
Winston-Salem, NC 27130

First Edition

Cover design by Mike Davis
www.mikedaviscreative.net

Author photo by Kat Lewis

Printed on acid-free paper
ISBN 978-1-941209-49-3

For Wynston and Alonzo,
my heart and my joy

The author wishes to thank the editors of the magazines in which these stories first appeared:

"All the Birds Vanish" *Passages North*

"Bait" *descant*

"Cast Again" *South Dakota Review*

"Gray Dogs" *SmokeLong Quarterly*

"High on the Divide" *damselfly press*

"The House Settling" *River City*

"The Stroke of Midnight" *Seattle Review*

"Thirsty" *Ascent*

"This Is History" *Green Mountains Review*

"Walk with the Animals" *Snake Nation Review*

"The Widow's Guide to Edible Mushrooms" *Marathon Literary Review*

CONTENTS

Thirsty   1

This Is History   19

The Good People of Great Falls   33

High on the Divide   53

Walk with the Animals   57

Bait   73

All the Birds Vanish   83

Gray Dogs   103

The Stroke of Midnight   107

Cast Again   125

The Widow's Guide to Edible Mushrooms   139

The House Settling   155

The issue with beginners…many of them are so eager to harvest wild mushrooms that when they find anything remotely close to a desirable mushroom, like a morel, they tend to fill in the blanks with what they want to see rather than what is actually there.

"Wild Mushrooms: What to Eat, What to Avoid"
by Tom Oder, *Mother Nature Network*

THIRSTY

I stayed in Gila Bend because I wanted my world so small that Roy would loom large for me again. I wanted him to fill me up the way he had when we'd first married, two years earlier, when the simple thud of his work boots on the front porch made me stop and smile and think *home.*

I could have believed that scummy motel room in Gila Bend to be some sort of home if I'd known my heart was in it. But all that I'd left behind in L.A. kept sliding between me and Roy like a glass door so slick you don't want to open it for fear of leaving evidence of your own sticky fingerprints.

What had I left behind? My rented house, a job sewing for a dressmaker who said she'd take me back for the holiday season, and a spiral notebook in which I recorded movie-star sightings, alphabetically, by first name. It started with Alan Alda at the California Pizza Kitchen in spring of 1988 and ended with who I thought was Yasmine Bleeth on Venice Beach. I'd also left behind nightclubs that never closed, and enough political scandals and murders to satisfy my secret lust for the sensational.

But those would all be waiting when I returned. Luisa was another matter altogether, and she's what I missed most, what

I couldn't explain to Roy. When he got a summer construction job in Gila Bend, Arizona, he begged me to come. He had it all worked out. His brother would rent the house, and he'd be making enough that I could take time off from work. He said we needed to get away, just the two of us, to work on our marriage, and I couldn't raise any reasonable objections, at least not without bringing Luisa into the equation. Our marriage had been dying by degrees, as my single friends stopped calling, as we'd come home from work too tired for sex or even conversation, as we started predicting what each other would say before it was said. Roy said that's just the way things happen, that you have to get through it, but that attitude seemed so dull and old-person to me.

But when he asked, I said yes. I thought there was something romantic about summer in a small town. I thought we just might work it all into the happy ending. Then I saw Gila Bend.

"Was that a town?" I asked, watching a strip of adobe houses recede in the rearview mirror.

"That was it, Sheila. And that's the site over there," Roy answered. He pointed to a nest of highway-repair equipment with several trailers circled round, like a wagon train protecting itself from something, maybe the vast desert itself.

We did a three-point turn on the highway and went back to find where we'd be staying. I noted two bars, one attached to a small grocery with a banner advertising *Cheap Fruit!*, which seemed, with its wide blue canopy over the doorway, to invite the loitering of three elderly men fanning themselves. Not far from the bars was a church complete with spire and cross, and scattered around the main drag were several stuccoed buildings tinged candy pink, apple green, and mostly a sad putty gray.

Two gas stations ate up the prime spots near the two motels, competing for tourists on their way to Yuma or Mexico or back to Phoenix. The Texaco was shiny red and black with slick new pumps and nozzles designed to prevent the escape of fumes. It seemed the obvious choice over Gabe's Gas which was directly across the street and next to the spaceage-designed motel where we were staying. The station had lost a few letters from its cracked marquee, and it stuttered *Ga Gas*. The place seemed deserted except for a batch of old cars rooted in and around the garage. The bright Pepsi machine painted with water drops bursting off the can seemed to move behind the heat waves rising from the pavement, like it was sweating and shivering at the same time.

There was no wind that day in mid-May, just the bleaching sun and me and Roy in an '89 Mazda. I looked around me and said, "God. I want to go home."

"Please, Sheila. You promised you'd try. And I can't get out of this job now." Roy turned off at the only motel with a swimming pool in its parking lot. But the pool hadn't been filled. The cracked blue paint baked into the concrete bottom, and an empty styrofoam cup stood perfectly upright in the center. I wondered if all the water had simply evaporated.

We got a room, "the best in the house," according to the chubby desk clerk whose name tag read *Albert*. The room wasn't altogether clean—scum in the sink, rust stains in the toilet. The bedspread was a gaudy pink-floral print, the kind my grandmother still used in her guest room, and the pictures on the wall were of coquettish senoritas and their lovers. I gulped down the tears I felt pinching the top of my throat, and I told Roy I'd get us unpacked while he checked in with his foreman.

I sat for a few minutes on the queen-sized bed thinking about calling Luisa, though I knew she wouldn't take a collect call, not from me. Not with her husband in charge of paying bills. He'd look at that number, call me right back, and maybe talk to Roy like he'd threatened before. I hung the clothes on wire hangers in the tiny closet and folded our socks and underwear, designating one night-table drawer for me and the other for my husband. Then I mixed it all up, socks in one drawer and underwear in the other.

When Roy returned, I was watching *Magnum, P.I.* reruns on a Yuma channel that came in fuzzy. "It's freezing in here," Roy complained when he took off his shirt. His nipples were hard as beads, and when he held the shirt to the overhead light, I could see the yellow sweat stains under the arms.

"Air conditioning."

"I *know* what it is. It's too damn cold." He snapped the switch off. "Where's the Clorox?"

Roy loved to sweat. It was part of what he liked about construction, especially when he ran the jackhammer that shook him to his bones. He believed it purged all the impurities from his body when the sweat came from so deep down. Roy may have loved to sweat, but he was disgusted by the stains it left. He soaked his shirts in a solution that was so strong it eventually ate away the shirt and left him stinking of cleaner instead of the musky smell I liked.

"The bleach is in the bathroom. I used some on the toilet."

Roy came out of the bathroom with a new T-shirt on. "Thanks for putting things away for me," he said. "I'm tired from driving." I hated driving, especially on the freeways, and I was grateful that he always did it, even when he didn't really want to. He leaned in toward me. "What are you up to now?"

"Writing letters." I expertly slid my hand over the legal pad I'd brought and instead showed him the ballpoint I'd swiped from the desk clerk. The pen stated in stamped gold type: *Bullhead City Gas—Best in the Southwest and That Ain't No Bull!*

Roy chuckled and stood in front of the television screen, blocking my view of Tom Selleck. "Who to?" he asked casually, putting me on guard with his seeming nonchalance.

"Friends. Mom. Luisa."

"Getting more hair tips?" I just nodded, and he leaned over and scrunched my already-frizzy bangs.

Luisa was our next-door neighbor. She permed my hair with solution that smelled as bad as Clorox. I was sometimes afraid that what happened to Roy's shirts would happen to my hair, but so far my head wasn't threadbare. And the risk seemed worth the feel of Luisa's firm fingers on my head, twisting the curling rods and massaging shampoo into my scalp. I sometimes think those fingers were responsible for everything that happened after. But I know better than to blame bodies that only do what comes natural. It's the rest of us—the brain, the secret heart, that deceives and justifies and generally messes things up.

"Say hi to Luisa for me. Hank too." Roy stretched out on the bed beside me and put his hands behind his head.

"I will," I answered, watching his face, a tight smile pinched on mine. He looked tired. Dark creases under his eyes and premature crow's-feet from all his work outdoors. He smiled back, with his mouth only, a mirror of my own expression. Then he pulled back the covers and crawled in.

"It's still a little cold in here," he explained before settling in for a nap.

We'd known Hank and Luisa for less than a year, since they moved into the house next to ours. Hank had a good job for the government, and he preferred Luisa to stay home with the baby, Billy, so she was always home on my days off. When she'd mentioned that she'd had some training at cosmetology school, I jumped on that. Perms are expensive, and the salons I can afford never do them right anyway.

I loved how gentle Luisa was on my scalp. She said my hair was baby fine and I shouldn't get perms, but I asked for them anyway. I liked that my hair kept slipping out of the curlers so that she would curse and roll each section again, and I would be treated to an extra half-hour of that gentle hair-tugging. Luisa said that I was too hard on my hair, that I should be more patient. When she watched me brush straight through a tangle, she gasped at the noise, like when I ripped out the seam on a dress. She wanted to color it blond but I thought of Roy's shirts and knew my hair wouldn't stand for bleach on top of L'Oreal home perms.

Our husbands occasionally got together to watch basketball, and Luisa and I talked about planting a flower garden between our driveways. On Thursdays, the days I had off from the dressmaker's, we used to go grocery shopping together. When we'd loaded the final bag from the car onto our kitchen tables, we'd part by kissing the air on either side of our faces and making silly smacking sounds like Hollywood starlets.

One afternoon our lips brushed. We both laughed and moved back, and I remember staring down at my feet and noticing that my big toenail was starting to split down the middle. I filled in the silence by asking to borrow a pair of toenail clippers.

"Toenail clippers?" She grunted as if she couldn't quite laugh and stared at my feet as I worked the blades around the nail. I thanked her and slinked back to my house, the offending piece of halved toenail clenched tightly in the palm of my hand until I could drop it in the wastebasket.

We shopped the next week, stocking up on fresh melon and store-brand baked beans at 99 cents a can. I helped Luisa inside with the last honeydew melon, and she sliced a hunk for each of us, a smaller piece for Billy, who just squeezed it with his fingers. We slurped at the melon, giggling as the juice dribbled down our chins, too fast for our tongues to catch.

At the door, in her cool front hallway decorated only with a glossy picture of the Virgin Mary, I instinctively moved my face closer to hers until I could nearly taste the sweetness of her breath. A drop of melon juice winked at the corner of her mouth when she smiled, and I could imagine my tongue lapping it off. But Luisa suddenly backed up and said in a bright voice, "Thanks, Sheila, for helping out. Same time next week?"

I nodded and walked home, hoping Roy would want baked beans for supper. The next Thursday, Luisa called to say she had other errands to run and couldn't get groceries with me. She had a similar excuse for the next two weeks, until one morning I watched from my kitchen window as she lifted groceries from her hatchback. Balancing Billy on one hip, she dropped a carton of eggs on the pavement and began to swear in her mother's Spanish. I rushed out and helped with the rest of the bags. She smiled gratefully but didn't say anything until she'd put Billy down for his nap. Then she invited me into the backyard for a glass of iced tea.

"I've missed you," she said quietly. "I've got no one to complain about Hank to." She grinned, and I confessed that I'd missed her too. We exchanged the usual intimacies of the foolish things our husbands had done, never mentioning the tension of her hallway and the honeydew melon, but when I stood to go home and start dinner, Luisa kissed me warmly on the cheek. I felt the wet print evaporate slowly as I approached my front door.

Something changed between us after that. We still shopped together, but afterwards, we laid out in the backyard and swapped childhood stories and sometimes rubbed suntan lotion on each other's shoulders. We laid out until the baby cried or Hank pulled up in the driveway, then we'd touch lips to cheeks, warm and solid, no more of that showy air-kissing.

Lip to lip seemed a natural next step. I think Luisa may have initiated it, but it doesn't matter. All that matters is we both got giggly and childish about it, and I felt a blooming in my belly that tickled and stung at the same time. And we became careless, so silly about exploring each other's mouths that we never heard Hank's car.

He was pissed.

He called me names that would have provoked Roy to knock him flat. But I wasn't about to tell Roy, and, as if Hank knew that, he threatened that if I came near his wife again, he'd go straight to my husband. Luisa started crying and screaming at him, and I could still hear their yelling when I went back to my own house. I wondered what the old lady in her garden across the alley thought.

I lay down on the bed with a cold washrag on my forehead though it was my stomach that ached most. When Roy came home and saw I didn't feel well, he made dinner—macaroni and cheese from scratch—and that just made me feel worse.

Luisa found me on my next day off and apologized. "Fuck Hank," she said, and before I could answer, she kissed me there in my house, brief and hard so I could feel teeth behind those lips. Then Luisa laughed and said that was how she and her sister had kissed their old widowed aunts at family gatherings to avoid tasting their breath. "They tasted like rancid coffee beans or sometimes strong bitter tea," she laughed. "That's why we always giggled when our mami told us to go kiss *las tias*."

I loved her stories, so even though I was nervous, I agreed to talking on the phone late at night, after our husbands had gone to bed. Luisa would sing me soft lullabies when I told her I couldn't sleep, and when she was feeling down and depressed about being stuck with a baby all day, I would list everything about her I liked, from the way she tucked her hair behind one ear to the fact that she could get really angry about politics. Sometimes, I'd look up at the clock and find that two hours had passed. My left ear would hurt where I'd pressed the phone tightly, and when I finally crawled under the covers with Roy, I had to massage the blood back into it.

I told Luisa about Roy's new job one night, and she said, "You're not going, are you?" When I said I might have to, she snapped, "No one has to do what they don't want to. Unless they're in jail or something."

"You don't want to stay with Hank," I pointed out, reminding her of previous conversations we'd had.

"I also want to be a good Catholic," she answered. "God wins." I heard the empty space of her yawn on the other end of the phone. "Do whatever you want," she finally said. "I couldn't care less, *mi querida*."

"That's a mean thing to say, Lu."

"And it's a mean thing to leave me now," she answered. "Have fun in the sun. Don't burn that white skin."

Roy had said the desert was beautiful at night, and he was right. After I rubbed his shoulders that first evening in Gila Bend, we took a walk out by the site. He wanted to show me where to find him in the early morning hours when the crew was trying to beat the heat. While we walked, hand in hand, Roy warned me about scorpions, how they crawled out at night, but I didn't care. I was looking at the sky, how black it was, how many stars. I'd never seen a sky like that in California.

"That's Phoenix." Roy pointed to a reddish glow in the north.

"Is it close?"

"About an hour. Maybe we can go when I get a few days off."

"I want to go now," I pouted, forgetting the sky and turning to that red smear on the horizon. "I don't think I can make it here. It's so . . . small."

"Sheila, please," was all he could say in that sad voice he saves for talking with me. When we walked back to the motel, I tried to watch for cactus and scorpions, but it was too dark, and I couldn't see what I was looking for.

Over the next two weeks, I read all my magazines twice, watched nearly a year's worth of *Magnum, P.I.* episodes and mailed three letters to Luisa. I wrote that I was going crazy with boredom. I wrote and told her all the things that I hadn't had a chance to say before we'd left. I admitted to being hurt and confused and I may have even said I was in love with her. While waiting for a reply, I spent my afternoons scouring the toilet and sink to get rid of the grime and make the room homier. Finally, I gave up on both Luisa and the rust stains.

Mostly I stayed indoors. Outside the temperature never fell below 90, and that was at night. Days it could top 115, and the air was so dry I felt my face would crack. I bought so much lotion at the local store that I soon knew the owner, Leonard, by name. He called me Thirsty and laughed at the way my skin slurped up so much lotion but never any color. He said I might be the whitest person he knew, and when I told him about watching *Magnum, P.I.,* he said I *was* the whitest person he knew. Then he showed me the new brand of moisturizer he'd ordered just for me. He said it came highly recommended from his mother-in-law and cost less.

One afternoon when Roy and I went to the store together to buy lunch meat, Leonard called out from the produce aisle, "Hey there, Thirsty." Roy thought he was flirting with me and later demanded to know what he'd meant by that "thirsty" bit. I tried to explain about the lotion and the sun, but I could see in his eyes that he didn't quite believe me.

He knew I was lonely, so he invited some of the crew guys to our room to play cards. Martin and Turo tried to be nice, telling me how cute I was and teasing me about what I did by myself in a motel room. I appreciated them trying, and I liked that they let me win a couple games of hearts, but I had this feeling that Roy had put them up to the whole evening. He kept prompting the conversation with awkward conversation starters like, "Turo's ex-wife liked the Beatles. Which Beatle is your favorite, Sheila?"

"The dead one," I mumbled.

Martin and Turo never came back after that night, preferring instead to go to Phoenix a few nights a week to check out the girly bars. Leonard was the only local who was very friendly to me, but I knew that neither his wife nor Roy would like me hanging around the store, so I didn't know where to go or what to do. The motel room was depressing and never clean enough for my comfort, and the Yuma channel didn't even carry the quality talk shows like *Oprah.* Besides, I was tired of watching different people mess up their lives in the same ways and pretend to figure it all out in the last ten minutes of the program.

I didn't like the idea of driving to Phoenix myself, and there was nowhere else to drive to, so I decided to spend time in the coffee shop attached to the motel. I'd only been there with Roy a few times on our weekly night out. Mostly we bought sandwich fixings to save money, and the desk clerk, Albert, let us use the microwave in the break room. Sometimes, though, Roy would treat me to dinner, and I'd order the chimichanga because I liked how the name sounded, so festive and exciting.

The day I went into the coffee shop alone, the waitress brought me the hot fudge sundae I'd been craving, and when she smoothed her tired hair behind one ear, I thought of Luisa.

"Is it always this hot?" I asked, trying to sound friendly.

The woman looked at me squinty-eyed. She was in her forties, her hair silver and black and full of split ends, and she was dressed in plain jeans and a loose cotton shirt. She didn't look much like a waitress.

"You're from the coast, right?" She leaned on the table and looked in my eyes.

"California."

"Well, Miss California, it's always hot in Arizona in the summer. It's just going to get worse, so you better buy an extra fan for that motel room." She turned quickly and started to clear coffee cups from a table behind me.

I brooded on this awhile, taking comfort in the sweet pools of fudge on my spoon. I licked at the ice cream slowly, trying to think my way out of three more months of long, hot boredom.

"Does it ever rain?" I turned to the waitress. She glanced up and sighed.

"When it rains in Gila Bend," she said slowly, "it pours." Then she went back to filling salt shakers, and she didn't say anything more, not even when I paid and left a too-big tip.

Roy told me to lay off the ice cream. It was another dry, hot evening and we'd made love for the first time in quite a while. He was used to the work now and wasn't so tired anymore, and I had begun to need him physically again, almost as if this marriage encounter in Nowhere, Arizona was working its magic. He had been so gentle, so right there with me, that my heart felt swollen, tender and fragile like one of the souffles in the *Ladies' Home Journal* I'd nabbed from the lobby.

Then he patted my thigh. He said, "Better lay off the ice cream."

"What?" I felt the slightest prick and the slow, painful deflating of something that had felt achingly good. He laughed and tickled me at the waist while I squirmed and begged him to stop.

"Admit it," he teased, fingers crouched over my belly. "Admit you've been spending my money on hot fudge sundaes."

I slapped his hand away, my skin suddenly sensitive to the pain of touch. "How did you know?"

"Charlotte told me."

"Oh." I hadn't realized Roy knew the waitress, but it made sense. When I'd mentioned my husband was working the crew, she'd opened up to me some, told me that her fiancé probably worked with Roy.

"I talk to her some on morning break. You probably aren't awake by then." He grinned and rolled on top of me, pinning me to show how strong he was.

I couldn't explain why, but I was hurt that Charlotte, who made the best sundae I'd ever eaten, who had begun listening to me pour out my troubles, who even gave me advice sometimes, talked to Roy too. I began to wonder if she'd only been nice to me because Roy was one of the boys.

"What else did Charlotte tell you?"

"She said you're a big tipper." Roy didn't look at me when he said this, so I waited for him to finish whatever point he wanted to make. "You know we can't afford that kind of expense."

"It's just a sundae!" I sat up, folding my arms protectively about me, suddenly angry and a bit spiteful.

"It's over twenty bucks a week," he said quietly. "Including tax and tip."

"Oh." I'd never added it up or thought about it. Hell, I didn't even eat the whole thing. But I didn't want to tell Roy that. It was his money I was eating up.

"I'll be better," I promised.

The next day a business-sized envelope from Luisa arrived. Albert knocked on my door at nine in the morning to give it to me. I was in a beastly mood and ready to take it out on him until I saw the return address. "Not before noon," I sighed. He shrugged and said it wasn't his fault the mail came so early. Then he went back to sweeping the parking lot, because there was no one for him to check out that morning.

I tore through the envelope so carelessly that I ripped the letter and had to piece it back together. I read it through twice, then went to the window and peeked out at Albert. I watched him bend slowly to pick up a beer can. His face was rosy and sweaty, and he seemed to be breathing hard. I watched him crumple the can in one thick fist then toss it like a free-throw at the garbage can. I quickly shut the curtain. I didn't want to see him miss.

I went to the cafe early that day. Charlotte looked surprised to see me.

"I need a sundae. Extra hot fudge," I announced, sliding into my favorite blue-vinyl booth.

"Isn't it a little early?" She sat across from me and asked if I wouldn't rather have something to drink, like coffee. I thought of how my breath would smell, rancid like Luisa's aunts, and I shook my head no. She studied my face and asked, "What's the matter?"

It was the first time she'd asked me about my troubles without my prompting her.

"Luisa's pregnant again." I turned to look out the window to where I could see the red dust clouds from the highway where the crew was working. Everything was bleached as bone, heat waves shimmering off the cars parked on the street. I suddenly wished I could go swimming, but I knew they wouldn't fill the pool. Albert said water was precious that year, too precious for tourist recreation. But when he told me, he seemed to regret it, and I imagined him in bright red swimming trunks, the elastic band hidden under his doughy fat. I imagined he would never leave the pool, because in water everyone is buoyant.

"Your friend from L.A. is having a baby? You should be happy for her." Charlotte stood and said we'd have a sundae on the house, to celebrate.

"But I'm not!" I must have yelled louder than I intended, because the teenage fry cook, Felipe, who preferred to be called Flip, looked out from the kitchen. Charlotte gave a short wave to show that everything was okay, and Flip disappeared. She sat down once more and rubbed at a spot on the table with a wetted index finger.

"Sorry," I mumbled. "It's just that she spends all her time on her first kid, and another one will keep her so crazy that she'll never have time to figure out what she wants." I paused, remembering that I was almost out of birth control pills and had no clue where to get refills. I was beginning to think I wouldn't need them anymore until that last night with Roy. "So, no, I'm not happy for her."

"I know," she replied. "I only said you should be. She's your friend, and if she's happy..." She gazed out the window, gone for a moment in some story of her own. I waited quietly, wishing she'd give a story back to me to make the exchange fair and equal, but she returned without revealing wherever she'd been. "Maybe you're just going stir-crazy. Like cabin fever in the desert. You should go somewhere. Phoenix maybe."

I looked into her small brown eyes, and she seemed really wise and kind at that moment. "Let's go together," I suggested. "Today."

Charlotte laughed. "Are you kidding? That only works in the movies. Tito would kill me if I walked on this job."

I sighed and looked out on the bleak desert. I noticed a small knot of men in hardhats approaching and recognized the swagger of Roy's long body.

"I better go," I said, standing, suddenly embarrassed. Charlotte watched me pick up the pieces of Luisa's letter and tuck them in my shorts pocket.

"Things will get better. July is the start of monsoon season. That'll be a change."

"Monsoons? Like in the jungle?"

"No," she answered. "Like in the desert. It's just a fancy name for a downpour. But hey, it's a change."

Roy had a few days off around the Fourth of July, so we hopped in the car for a trip to Phoenix. He was brown and lean and happier than I remembered seeing him. In the car, Roy sang along to an oldies station, while I kept looking down at my legs, wondering how they ever got so white. When I raised my sunglasses to study them, they looked like lumps of bread dough that threatened to never stop rising. I poked at them, half-hoping they'd deflate, but all I got for my trouble was a few red spots.

I was so eager to get to Phoenix, I paid no attention to the desert, even when Roy pointed out the gnarled Joshua trees and what he thought was a wolf. Instead, I fidgeted with the vents and the AC and scanned through all the radio stations twice. Roy filled me in on the progress of road expansion in Gila Bend. I wasn't interested; I figured the road we were on was expanding somewhere better. But once we reached the outskirts—Sun City West where all the retirees lived—I felt my heart tighten. Everything was hot, shiny metal and asphalt.

We ate at a Taco Grande in the city and asked the employees where we should visit. They suggested Planet Hollywood, the malls in Scottsdale, museums, all the kinds of places I thought I missed. One older lady said the view from South Mountain was a good place to start, and I wrote directions on a napkin, mostly so I wouldn't stare at the purple cancer scabs on her nose. Then I made Roy drive us there.

We drove into the desert just south of the sprawling city, up a winding road. We parked at the top and walked to the guardrails. In the midday heat, we watched in silence as the air over the city shimmered, like a mirage in all directions. Yellow smog hugged the horizon, and the cars on the freeway were just glints of color. The only sound was the wind through the brush, and I was enjoying it until Roy opened his mouth.

"Sheila," he said. "I have a surprise."

"What?" The last time he'd said that, he'd handed me a diamond ring, quarter-carat. I'd been mesmerized by its shine, reached for it like a baby or a greedy, scavenging crow.

"I got an offer to work in Phoenix in the winter. We can leave L.A. behind and start over here. It's supposed to be especially beautiful in December. We'll get a house with a pool this time, and we'll keep it filled." He winked. "You could open your Christmas presents in a bikini."

I turned to look at him and saw that he was beaming, proud of what he could offer. A trail of sweat ran down his temple, but it didn't seem to bother him. I smiled at his enthusiasm. He was offering a fresh start, exactly what I wanted, but I didn't know how I could start with him again with the secret of Luisa behind every move I made, like some ghost haunting me. And as much as I wanted my pool to always be full, I worried that, in a city built on desert, Roy couldn't keep good on that promise.

"Let's wait and see," I whispered, the sound lost in the wind. I said it again, louder this time, but Roy was already back at the car, flicking rocks from the tire with the tip of the ignition key. When I went to him, to try to explain why it wouldn't work, he looked past me, out at the city, then said something I couldn't quite catch.

"What?" I leaned in closer, and a spray of wind-thrown dust stung my cheek.

"She never really loved you. You were a diversion. Can't you see that?"

I sucked in my breath and put my hand to my face to wipe the grit away, carefully, so I wouldn't get anything in my eyes.

Right then I understood. Not about what Roy had said, because I still think he's wrong on that count. But I understood what he knew and what he'd done. Maybe Hank had blabbed or Roy had guessed. It didn't matter. What mattered was that he hadn't thrown me aside or insisted I choose. He'd manipulated me away from her, and for that I felt somewhat betrayed. But I was in no position to be indignant about betrayals.

Roy had been there as always, holding his secret until the time was right, earning his place back with walks in the desert, another try at lovemaking, more empty time than I knew how to fill, and even the gentle complaints about my habits that showed me he was still and always would be Roy. I'd been too dumb, too caught up in my own drama, to recognize the quieter shadows of love.

We got back in the car, and the wind slammed my door harder than I would have meant. All the way back down the winding mountain road, I kept sneaking looks at him, trying to remember who he was and how I'd come to forget. He drove slowly, looking my way and smiling tentatively once or twice, but never when negotiating a curve, never when he needed his eyes on the road. Roy has always been a careful man.

THIS IS HISTORY

T-Minus 3 hours

We went as a family to see the smokestack get blown sky-high. We went as a family though our motives and emotions were distinctly individual. My mother grieved the destruction as though it were the last bastion of her family's identity. My grandfather had worked for the Anaconda Copper Company for nearly thirty years, from laborer in the Butte mines to smelting foreman in Great Falls, where the family had moved when my mother was twelve, my age. The company had finally bellied up in 1980, and now they wanted to knock down the stack for safety purposes. City engineers were convinced the whole 506-foot smokestack would come crumbling down any day if it weren't scheduled for immediate demolition. Structural weaknesses, they claimed.

My mother had been on the citywide campaign called SOS (Save Our Stack), selling T-shirts to raise funds to keep the thing standing as a monument. But to what? The industry that made the Butte Copper Kings rich at the turn of the century and left the land raped and polluted just a few decades later? I would argue this in my college years, partly because I believed it in my newfound liberal reactions, and partly because the demolition still bothered my mother years after the fact, and what daughter doesn't seek to nettle her mother just a bit? But the truth is nobody knew then why they wanted to keep the stack any more than they knew fifteen years later why they lobbied so hard to preserve the defunct 10th Street Bridge, a stone bridge that threatened to collapse under the weight of a single squawking seagull. Great Falls wanted to keep its past because it was past, reminder of a glory day that never really was. My mother was susceptible to fantasies of golden pasts and golden futures that would erase the daily shin-banging and toe-stubbing of the present. It's why she became such a fundamentalist when my father finally left us—a Second Coming is too much to resist in a world where chances are few.

Besides, she felt a loyalty to her father and all her uncles and cousins who had been able to make a living in the West thanks to Anaconda Copper, never mind that most of them had died early deaths, her father only fifty-two when he succumbed to a strange form of lung cancer. My father simply attributed my mother's new enthusiasm for saving this symbol of the working class to her job at Montana Power. "They're corrupting you," he'd joke, though the joke was soon threadbare and my mother stopped responding to it and started her own secret savings account with part of the check she earned each month.

She was wearing one of the SOS T-shirts that morning when we set out to secure a good place from which to watch the stack blow. It was just past seven, and the demolition wasn't scheduled until ten, but there were already cars lining River Drive as we looped around to the baseball diamond just above the road. Ben was holding the donuts we'd picked up from the IGA, and he kept sliding his finger under the lid to dig at the chocolate frosting on the nearest donut. I noticed, but for once didn't tattle. I was in too good a mood to quibble, thrilled at the thought of seeing something blasted to dust. And Ben, subject to teenage mood swings and usually crabby when wakened before noon, was gleeful.

We parked on a grassy hill, still wet with dew, and my father announced as he pulled the emergency brake, "Two hours, forty-nine minutes until mass destruction." Then he turned in his seat and said, "Chocolate donut, please."

"You can have the maple bar," Ben offered.

"Chocolate. I picked it out myself."

"Yeah, well, I thought it was mine." Ben held up the fat greasy ring with a plaster of chipped chocolate on it. The nicks looked distinctly like the moons of his now-brown fingernails.

"Gross," I piped in.

My father didn't say anything, just grimaced and picked up the maple bar, holding it to the sunlight to be sure it wasn't marred. When he bit into it, tan flecks nested in the beard he'd been growing for two weeks. My mother hated the stubble, said it wasn't very Presbyterian.

Now she was humming to herself, "Good Morning Sunshine" I think it was. I remember because I was surprised that she could be so cheery in the hours before the loss of what she'd tried to save. There was the white T-shirt with the sketch of the large two-toned stack and the red letters *SOS* and her nipples raised because she wasn't wearing a jacket like the rest of us and spring mornings in Montana are cold. I noticed the cold nipples because I was still breast-conscious, having just started wearing a training bra that school year. The presence of nipples, never noticeable under the thick padding of my first bras, embarrassed me, especially because I knew my mother would be embarrassed if she knew.

"Can you turn on the heat, Dad?"

"It'll warm up soon enough," he answered, finishing a last bite of donut and watching the cars mill around the river area, looking for prime parking. It was worse than the Holiday Mall Shopping Center at Christmas, and my father was privately gloating that we'd beat the rush. Of course that meant we had a lot of time to kill, and after half an hour in the car watching traffic and the slow melt of frost whiskers on our car, we were all restless.

My mother had brought a book, a Christian romance like the kind she read on her lunch breaks, tucked into her small knit purse as if it, and not her hard nipples, was the embarrassment. Ben had assured me there was nothing good in those books, and my best friend Paula, who was reading illicit Judy Blume books during school, concurred.

"You wanna read something sexy, read this," she'd said, shoving a tatty paperback at me. On the cover was a heart-shaped locket, and in it a pretty young woman in a sweater with a cute boy behind her. It looked romantic, so I opened the cover and the book fell open to a page that had been highlighted in a garish orange.

"Ick," I'd said, my eyes fixed on the nasty words on the glowing page.

"You think that's bad?" Paula had giggled. "Wait 'til you get to the part where he names his penis Ralph." Just like that I'd entered a world where men named their private parts. For weeks after, I'd wanted to ask Ben about it, but I knew he would have laughed and laughed as if Paula had made it up. And I really couldn't trust what Paula had made up or not.

I wished I had something to read that May morning at the end of my sixth-grade year. Ben and my father had brought an old football to toss, and their game had quickly come to involve two young air force men who'd parked down the lane from us. I could hear them grunting and calling out cheers from the baseball field where the Great Falls Dodgers usually played.

My mother leaned her seat back, creasing the small book into her lap. "Do you have enough legroom, Mouse?"

"Yes," I said, pleased she'd used my new nickname. "Eve" was too burdensome a name in a religious family, and I'd always had a fondness for Mickey Mouse, which may be why I chose that for a nickname. "But I'm bored already."

"Didn't you bring anything? I told you it would be a while." Her eyes never seemed to leave the page as she talked to me, so I assumed she was at a really good part.

"You could read to me," I suggested.

She paused, and from that hesitation I expected some scoffing dismissal, but then she started to read in a loud, clear, and somewhat dramatic voice.

"Pam rushed through the house, looking for David, but a little voice in her head or an angel on her shoulder told her he wasn't there. She'd prayed she would find him waiting for her, maybe even starting a nice chicken dinner, but God had let her down this time, she thought."

"Wow," I said, stretching my legs onto Ben's side of the backseat. "Where did David go?" I imagined poor Pam thawing the chicken alone while David caroused in a whorehouse. The last time I'd slept over at Paula's one of her brothers was watching *The Best Little Whorehouse in Texas*, and I knew it was a very bad place for good men to be.

"He's staying with his mother. David became a Christian after they were married, and he wants Pam to join the church so they won't be unevenly yoked." My mother said this so matter-of-factly that I started to giggle. I heard "yoke" and thought egg yolk, and I was picturing Pam and David getting egged by unbelievers, thick orange goop sliding down their faces. I was giggling hard by the time my mother turned in her seat and raised her voice.

"That's not funny!" she snapped.

I was shocked into abrupt silence. She was obviously sensitive on this yoke issue, and I mumbled an apology though I didn't think I'd done anything wrong. I thought at the time she just didn't like her reading made fun of, and I could identify. Ben was forever mocking my *Young Miss* magazines, sneering "Young Mouse reads Young Miss." And though his taunts were harmless, and basically stupid, I got mad and tried to kick him more than once.

Now I wonder if my mother wasn't projecting her own life into the story. Only she was David and, ironically, my father, the pastor, was Pam. He was already pulling away from his Christian life, begging off more and more pastorly duties. At least he must have been. He left for Ireland that summer, a couple of months after the stack blew, after Ben's sixteenth birthday. But on that day I assumed, as children do, that I'd stepped over yet another invisible line in a world of rights and wrongs that rarely made rational sense.

She went back to reading the book silently, and after a few more pages, she let it fall shut, tucked it back in her knit bag. "Let's take a walk or something," she suggested kindly, a sudden turnabout from the snarl of minutes earlier.

"Sure." I'd worn sandals and would get my feet wet in the cold dew, but I couldn't bear feeling cramped in the car while my father and brother ran and chased a football. "Do you want to borrow my coat?"

"It's a little small for me, don't you think?" She opened her door and inhaled deeply, exaggerating the exhaled "aaaahs" like a person in a commercial advertising spring-fresh scent laundry detergent.

"You'd be surprised. I'm still growing."

"Yes, you are. Soon you'll be marrying some boy from the church, and I'll be a grandmother before I even know how to be a mother."

"Geez," I said, though she didn't like that word, claiming it was really an abbreviation for "Jesus" which was taking the Lord's name in vain, an obvious sin. "You're a good mom anyway," I added, trying to gloss over my slip-up and at the same time divert her from these strange moments when she spoke as though both of our lives were planned out, practically over, and ultimately disappointing.

We stepped into the new grass growing on the mound where my father had parked, taking care not to let our doors bump the Chrysler that had pulled up next to us. Most of the grassy hill was covered with cars winking glints of color in the morning slant of sun. The sky was a rich blue, and a few high clouds skidded on the air. I saw a jet trail to the east where the Air Force base was located just a few miles away, and though the air was still brisk and my mother's nipples would still be on display, I knew it was going to be a splendid spring day, and I felt that surge in the gut that made me want to run, my arms back like a goose on takeoff. Then I remembered the sandals. They were my Easter sandals, still new (but no longer so crisply white) and uncomfortable enough that I wouldn't be running anywhere that morning. I settled for tiptoeing through the grass, trying not to get too wet.

My mother had prayed for a storm. The night before, when we were saying prayers before a dinner of macaroni and meatballs, the kind I liked with little onion crescents, she'd added to my father's usual prayer: "And God, please bring bad weather so the stack can't be destroyed." My father had told her, mostly for the spiritual education of Ben and myself, that God didn't answer those kinds of prayers. But we all fell silent when the evening news came on and the pink-cheeked weatherman predicted the warmest, clearest day of the spring. It seemed that in spiritual matters my father and God were on the same side. My father went to bed without a word, seemingly gracious in his victory, but the next morning as he was rousing Ben, he kept repeating that he hadn't seen such a beautiful day in months.

He was right, but that didn't change the fact that the very glory of the day was spiting my mother. She was terse as we picked out donuts, arguing for cream filling instead of jelly for no good reason, and she prickled with tension until we were riding in the car and the sun warmed her face as she leaned against the window, staring out onto wheat fields along the east edge of Great Falls. Then I saw her shoulders visibly relax and give an inch to gravity. Her shoulder-length hair, dark brown with strands of silver, curled over the side of the seat so I could almost touch it from where I sat. She let her eyes roam over the passing fields that were still dead, none of the rich black earth tilled over quite yet. She sighed a few times, those contented sighs that told me she knew that whether the Anaconda stack was demolished or not, spring was here. Some form of renewal and hope was whispering on the horizon, and maybe that would be enough to get her through the day, the week, the year.

My mother wasn't very vocal about her attachment to the huge brown and black smokestack that looked like a giant upright cigar, a Freudian fantasy of immense proportion. I imagine she may have been more expressive with my father, especially just before he left the country and our family. But knowing my mother as I do now, I can see all the ways in which that defunct smoke belcher came to represent her roots, roots that were threatened by my father's privileged East Coast background. He was book-educated at a college then seminary in Boston, and it was a sense of adventure that brought the young Presbyterian minister to work as an assistant pastor in Great Falls, Montana.

He hadn't meant to stay long, maybe a couple of years at most, as long as it took to learn to ride a horse the way he'd always seen in the Westerns. Then he'd met my mother and, enchanted by the girlishness that hid her strong ambitions, he'd married her. He'd waited for her to tire of her small life, trying to tempt her East with stories of Broadway and galleries and all the things he wanted to show her. But she wanted to raise her children near her family and to be the wife of a head pastor. Her first wish was coming true.

By the time we were anxiously awaiting the demolition of the Anaconda Smokestack, he'd already turned down two chances to head the small congregation, and the church had recently brought in a head pastor from Sacramento, much to my mother's chagrin. I didn't care; Pastor Ron was handsome and cheery and still single, which intrigued Paula who, being Catholic, complained she never had anyone young or available to admire in her church. I occasionally made up things about Pastor Ron, elaborating how he'd held my hand in the handshake just a bit longer than necessary. Paula believed me under the complex code that young girls have about never undercutting someone else's sense of self-importance, however ridiculous the claim. I had few opportunities to show her up, so I took all I could get.

T-Minus 1 hour

Ben and our father returned from their ball game, sweaty and teasing each other with an easy camaraderie of which I was instantly jealous. My mother and I had picked spring wild flowers, some of which hadn't even opened their faces to the sun yet. I didn't mind the cowslips and brown-eyed Susans we'd collected, but somehow they reminded me that I had been dumb enough to wear the sandals that restricted my activities to ones like gathering flowers, and for that reason I resented it, resented the very flowers themselves.

"Hey, Mouse, what do you have there?" Ben asked, placing a warm and slightly sticky palm on the back of my neck.

"Flowers," I answered in as flat a voice as I could manage, my protection against the possibility that he would call me a "pansy" and try to steal them from me to crush in his wide hand.

"Cool." Ben plucked a daisy from my fist and set it gingerly behind his ear. He laughed and scruffed my hair and didn't remove the flower. It stayed there until some time after the explosion when it probably just flitted away, unnoticed in the wind that was always blowing through the city.

Ben's easiness that morning was unfamiliar to me. Though we'd been fairly close as younger children, when he reached puberty he'd begun using me as the psychological and sometimes literal punching bag for his every adolescent grievance. The times he was generous and big-brotherly I grew suspicious, afraid I would come to enjoy our closeness and then have it whisked out from under me. Childhood is a lot like that. Despite people's nostalgic claims on it, childhood is horror, the bewilderment of inexplicable losses before one has come to acknowledge that's just the way things are. I think of the Disney movies I watched where good triumphed after a struggle with evil, where marriages were happily ever after, and I'm not surprised that so many people grow up expecting security and suffer extended adolescences into their twenties, even thirties and beyond. My parents grew up on the Bible, which is probably worse than Disney, because although the rapes, murders, adultery, and unhappy endings are there, everyone wills them out of awareness, the only way an adult can maintain the illusions of childhood.

That morning before the stack blew is so golden in memory. Despite my restrictive sandals, despite my jealousy of how close my brother and father seemed, I remember that hour before destruction as an idyllic spring morning, a breakfast picnic of fat donuts among wild flowers, the magical risk of dynamite and danger. Ben introduced me to the two airmen he'd played football with, and one of them, a thin pale man with a close-cropped mustache, gave me a piece of bubble gum and offered to let us watch the explosion from the roof of his truck. We listened to his stereo for a while because the local radio station was playing songs in tribute to the event at hand, tunes like "Eve of Destruction" and "Disco Inferno," and Ben asked all kinds of questions about the truck. He would turn sixteen that summer, and my father had agreed to let him get his driver's license and a job so he could save money for a car.

"You two want to take a spin in the truck?" the man asked in a thick and friendly voice.

His friend piped in, "I can hold our parking space with these lawn chairs." He snapped two canvas chairs open and tried to balance them on the rocky ground, bending one aluminum tube in the process.

"No thanks," Ben answered for both of us. "We've got to get back to our parents." He looked from his digital watch to the truck and finally tugged on my sleeve. "C'mon, Mouse."

"Well, have fun watching her blow," the mustached man called. His buddy giggled.

I was relieved to follow my brother, having heard too many stories about men who lure children into cars. I wasn't exactly sure what happened after that, only that they were never heard from again. A boogieman story for my generation. When I remembered that they used candy to get children, I spit my neon-pink gum into the grass. Then I felt guilty. My father would say I was ruining nature, and my mother would repeat her dictum, "What goes around, comes around." All that day I would be careful not to step in gum, fearful of what goes around.

T-Minus 9 minutes

When we returned to the car, my parents were gently arguing. I could tell from their tone of voice that it was really a discussion and nothing to worry about, so I stood behind my mother and leaned my head on her back.

"You just don't understand what copper means to this area, Jonathan. Every time you spit on that smokestack, you spit on my family."

"Not that again? The big bad Easterner and his power play to crush the Western spirit. Ooooh." My father shivered in mock fright and my mother lightly smacked his arm before turning to us.

"You've got less than ten minutes left to admire her." She looked across the river to where the stack stood as it had for years, stolid and smokeless. We couldn't even tell if the dynamite experts had left the area yet, and to this day I can't figure why my mother refers to that stack as "her." Freudian psychology or even the lesser cognitive skill of sight and comparison should have eliminated the feminine pronouns altogether, but to my mother the smokestack was like a ship, say the Titanic, immense and unsinkable as she may have imagined herself, and thus a "she."

We all leaned against the hood of the car, and I propped my sandals, streaked with grass stains, on the railing that separated our parking area from River Drive. The cars had stopped moving, because everyone knew the time was at hand, and the police had blocked off the road from Giant Springs to the 14th Street Bridge. People were celebrating already, not the event itself, but the fact that Great Falls was having an event besides the annual Charles Russell Art Auction. I saw young couples stoking portable barbecues, families still playing frisbee as though a bell would alarm them to look in the right direction at the right time, and a knot of young men not much older than Ben sneaking drinks of something from the trunk of a Mustang.

"It's only ten in the morning," my father said, shocked. He turned my head back to face the little hill where the stack still stood.

"Oh, Jonathan." My mother's voice was full of disappointment, and for a moment I wondered if I'd done something wrong. It was the same tone she'd used to say my name when my fourth-grade teacher told her I'd cheated on a math test. "I forgot the camera."

"Well," my father replied, stumped for words as if still shocked over the boys drinking, "We can frame whatever they run in tomorrow's *Tribune.*"

Ben piped in, "That's not the same." He grunted in disgust and started popping the heads off dandelions, then turned back to my mother. I saw that the flower was still tucked behind his ear, and I wondered why the airmen hadn't teased him about it. "Why do *you* want a picture of it anyway?"

She deflected the criticism well, simply saying, "This is history, Ben."

And so I braced myself for history, sneaking looks at everyone else's watches, since I'd broken my Mickey Mouse one after falling from the monkey bars at school. None of the functional watches were synchronized, so when my father's, the fastest one, marked ten, we all stared hard at the stack as if willing it to disappear. Nothing. No movement, almost no sound except birds singing and an occasional child's shout. We were all too scared of missing the explosion to look down at our wrists again, though my mother later claimed that the destruction went by her watch, exactly on the mark.

Impact

We saw it before we heard anything. Sudden long curls of smoke and ash tumbling earthward, like a Rapunzel gone gray from waiting for this very moment, then an earthquake rumbling punctuated by cracks and snaps and waves of pressure against my sternum. Then the cheering. Voices hooting and screaming, hands held high and clapping. And as the dust began to clear, a vision came into sight that set off a new, wilder round of applause.

Half of the stack remained. Like a jagged finger pointing to heaven, the base, extending all the way up the right side of the Anaconda smokestack, was still standing. And people were screaming and clapping each other on the back as if they realized that this was what they really wanted after all, a failed attempt to wipe out history.

My mother hugged me, pressing my face into her T-shirt so that my cheek was right against the drawing of the stack. I hugged her back and watched as Ben leapt up and down, whooping, and my father just stared at the smoking wreck across the river, a wry smile on his face, like this had been a little joke on God's part, something to put him in his place.

We didn't stay for the second explosion, the one that would finally reduce the great stack to a pile of dust and rubble. Someone would try to sell vials of dust from the site, the way bottles of ash from Mt. St. Helen's were packaged when the volcano smeared a thin layer of itself all over Great Falls two years earlier. But nobody was buying this time. The moment had passed, the stack was gone, and there was already talk of expanding the golf course into the site.

On the slow drive home, jammed among the other cars leaving the scene, we listened to the local radio station, a rock 'n' roll station both my parents openly despised. The disc jockeys were rotating a new set of songs, starting with "I Will Survive." Ben and I sang the chorus together while my parents patiently gazed out at the river and the greening fields, inscrutable smiles on their faces. My mother joined in the song once she got the lyrics, and my father, used to the tempo of hymns, bungled his way through the rapid disco beat. As a family we sang and studied the land for signs that summer was really on its way. We sang with the earnest lungs of believers.

THE GOOD PEOPLE OF GREAT FALLS

He listened to those words he'd stopped believing long ago: "Nobody blames you." His boss clapped a hand on his shoulder, and Brendan flinched. "But now you've got to prove your character. You have to help us."

He studied the table before him, ghostly semi-circles where his bleach-soaked rag—"Call them *towels*," insisted the boss's wife—had passed half an hour earlier. A missed scab of food marred the surface, something bland and colorless as jack cheese or dried mayo. Usually meticulous, he'd been shaken since Dennis greeted him at the start of his shift with the grim news: "Money's come up missing on your closing shift."

Debbie, Dennis's wife and the deli's co-owner, had raked the perfectly polished nails of her fingers through strands of her long, red hair while Brendan explained—truthfully—that he knew nothing about it. She'd stared straight through him, eyes burning, ready to exact vigilante justice then and there while Dennis had only shaken his head sadly, good cop to her bad. "Brendan," he'd said softly. "We took you in when no one else would."

True. He'd applied everywhere for work after high school. Thought it would be easy because while most of his classmates

were leaving for college or the armed forces, he was staying in town,
available to work any hours. He'd started with places he thought
he'd like: Pacific Steel, Poulsen's Lumber, Scheel's Sporting Goods.
But Great Falls, Montana, population steady at 55,000 for over
twenty years, was still too small, and as soon as he showed up for
an interview, he noted the confusion on the manager's face—*How
do I know this boy?*—followed by the inevitable flash of
recognition. And the job dried up, just like that. The woman at the
recycling center had even said when he'd called back a few days
later that he was overqualified. Overqualified to sort sticky pop
cans from tin! When Dennis had hired him at the deli in the mall,
he'd assumed he'd gone unrecognized until his boss had poured
himself a diet Dr. Pepper and said out of the blue and after a small
burp, "I believe in second chances." And his look said, yes, of course
he read the papers and watched the local news. "Sometimes we get
mixed-up with the wrong people is all."

By then he had given up explaining. "If you're innocent,
you don't *have* to explain," one detective had suggested when
Brendan sat at their small table, his knees knocking the
underside, words tangling and snagging in his mouth. He'd
simply been grateful for second chances and had worked like a
dog for Dennis and his wife these last four months. Now this.

"When do you work next? Thursday? We'll have Officer
Yellowrobe set you up for the sting that afternoon."

Brendan nodded and scraped the dried food with a chipped
thumbnail. The slush machine whirred, the swirl of its red, icy
guts visible through a round glass panel like a washing machine.
Atop the machine, bolted to the mixing rod, was a model Ford
Thunderbird, mint green, adorned with photos of Dennis and
Debbie hamming it up, bug-eyed with their tongues protruding
lizard-like. The car bucked and rotated. He listened to Debbie
in her brightest voice convincing a young woman whose three
grubby children were fighting over a single cherry slush to buy
one of their frozen pizzas for only $5. Brendan knew that the
pizzas were mismatched puzzles of slices that didn't sell but
sagged late in the day under the heat lamps, cheese coagulated,

pepperoni edges hopelessly shriveled. He put the Frankenpizzas together on cardboard rounds every night, wrapped them in cellophane, and popped them in the deep freeze. If there was one thing his bosses could complain about regarding his work it was that he didn't push the pizza deal. Guilty as charged. He wouldn't feed that garbage to his Rottweiler, and Rico was not known for his discriminating tastes.

Dennis sighed, always more buddy than boss, and shrugged. The cash register chirped Debbie's success. "I can understand letting Charlene use the employee bathroom, but it wasn't smart thinking. We fired her for a reason."

"I didn't know," Brendan repeated. "She told me she quit to pursue her acting career."

"Because there are so many casting agents in Montana? Come on." Dennis, a one-time theater major who'd had bit roles in local productions, leaned in and added softly, "Admit it. She's so fucking beautiful, you would have given her the whole cash register if she'd asked."

Also guilty as charged. He knew people who described their eye color as green, but he never believed it again after that Saturday when Debbie had grumbled that he was in charge of training the new employee because *somebody* had to take care of the books. And there was Charlene, stunning eyes the color of spring grass, and that tiny, coy smile painted a frosty plum. She was almost as tall as him, and even then he thought she could be a movie star. She had laughed, warm and throaty, at every instruction he gave until he too was chuckling at the absurdity that fries should get two shakes of the salt shaker, no more, no less. Charlene, he noted, always shook four times in a cute little rhythm like she was practicing with maracas.

"Good-looking or not," Dennis reminded him. "You've got to catch her red-handed. Or it's going to look bad for you."

When Brendan walked into the kitchen that evening, his mother was frying minute steaks, a juice glass full of zinfandel precariously placed at the edge of the counter.

"I hope you're not marinating our dinner with that."

"What? That's not how they fix gourmet food at the mall?" She took a gulp, wiped her mouth on the shoulder of her blouse, and stepped back as the meat snapped and sizzled in the pan. So it was going to be one of those nights.

"Where's Rico?" The dog was usually at the door before he'd finished opening it, his eager tongue attacking through the first crack.

"You ask about the dog before your father," his mother observed, pursing her lips.

"Where's Rick-o?" He'd stopped insisting on *step*father. She always came back with "The only father you've known." No arguing that.

"Ha ha. Should collar that one too. Rick's at Bible study." She lowered the heat on the steaks and turned an expectant face his way.

"*Bible study?*"

"My thoughts exactly," his mother mumbled. She finished the wine and set the glass down with a clunk that startled them both.

"Is that the name of a new bar or something?" He thought he detected a flash of amusement in his mother's eyes, but she said nothing. "So where's Rico?" Surely the smell of frying meat would have lured him out.

"Stop with the goddamned dog for a minute. Don't you want to know *why* your father is at Bible study?"

"Because you're damning God and my dog?" Her eyes narrowed and her nostrils flared. "Look, Mom, I had a bad day. I don't want to—" His mother cut him off with an angry flip of her hand.

"He has decided that this family is going to hell. He's going to *save* us through the power of prayer!" Spittle sprayed from her plosive "p"s, and Brendan backed off to retrieve the wine bottle from the fridge. He refilled her glass while she sputtered about how Rick seemed bent, *hell*-bent, on her personal embarrassment. "Laura Dermott goes to that same church you know." When he shrugged, no clue who she meant or why it mattered, she swallowed a mouthful of wine then threw the rest on the steaks. They both watched the crimson drops hiss, steam, disappear. "Food's done."

Brendan found Rico tied to the railing on the back porch, pacing the same four feet of trampled lawn, and knew that he must have escaped again. "Hey, Houdini!" The dog whined and drooled at his approach, leaping up on his back paws and rotating the useless propeller of his stubby tail. Brendan never thought he'd love a dog so much. What had started as a promise to a friend, a last-ditch play at loyalty, had turned to a spot of bright joy, a reason to come home at night. Still, Rico was a major bone of contention, no pun intended, between him and his mother.

"You would still do anything for that sick son-of-a-bitch, wouldn't you?" she'd snarled when he brought the dog home and explained the favor Toby had asked. Even his milder stepfather had given him a rare look of disgust.

"Five to ten years," Rick had said slowly. "The dog probably won't be alive when he gets out."

"That could have been you!" his mother had shouted. "And you want his *dog*? Like some *memento*?" She'd wept then, submitting to Rick's ministrations, and Brendan had stood alone, silently wondering why everyone believed he'd made some lucky escape when he hadn't done anything wrong. He'd been sitting in the front passenger seat, drinking a Big Gulp Mountain Dew. That wasn't against the law. And the dog was riding along, straining toward the window, seeking the wind in his face. Toby claimed his mother would have had Rico shot just because she couldn't shoot her own son, and it looked like his mother felt the same.

"Stay away from the neighbor's cats," he whispered into Rico's ear as he slipped the chain from his collar.

That Thursday morning Brendan was up early, nervous about the sting, or *potential* sting, given that his success depended on whether Charlene showed at all. She knew he worked, she'd even suggested, as she had once before, that they go out afterward for a drink, apparently unaware that he was still underage.

Rick was already at the breakfast table, head bowed over a plate of toast, his usual cup of black coffee cooling beside him. Brendan thought he was praying, but he was peering closely at the whole-grain slices.

"These damn flaxseeds look like bugs."

"Are born-again Christians allowed to cuss?" Brendan swigged freely from the orange juice carton, his parents having decided one day that their stomachs were too sensitive for all that acid. They'd cut out tomato sauce too, until his mother had learned that the alfredo she'd switched to was fattening. Now, no pasta at all.

Rick looked up in surprise. "I've been praying is all. Lots of people do that. No one said anything about born-again, though to hear your mother you'd think I was passing out pamphlets in front of the house."

"*She's* gone off the deep end then?"

Rick sipped his coffee and licked his lips before speaking. "A year ago she imagined you'd be in college in Bozeman by now. She'd already bought a set of sheets for your dorm bed."

"That isn't exactly normal." He wondered if they were a special, irresistible purchase that had screamed of his individual style or just ordinary sheets she'd seen on sale in Target.

"Then I won't mention the rocking horse she's tucked away for your first child."

"What?"

"Forget it. The point is we're all suffering. We need to find a way to cope, and your mother has her yoga."

"And you have prayer?"

"Something like that."

The sound of indignant barking echoed into the kitchen, and Brendan realized it was Rico's. "Damn it, why does someone keep tying him up?" He had the back door unlocked, ready to rescue his dog, when Rick interrupted.

"The dog stays tied."

"Why?" Fury surged in his gut and collapsed, nowhere to go.

"He's been a menace to the neighborhood, Brendan. The Tabers will call Animal Control next time they see him."

"The Tabers are assholes."

"I can't disagree there." They'd reported his uncut grass to the city, and now Rick mowed religiously every weekend, whether it had rained or not, returning to the house sweaty, peppered with tiny grass bits, and in a foul mood. And he wouldn't let anyone else do the lawn. It had become his personal cross to bear. "But Rico killed a kitten yesterday."

"Bullshit!"

"Stop it." Rick glanced at the clock and stood to clear his dishes. "I said they were mistaken. I said Rico had been in the yard all day and I knew because I'd come home at lunch and walked him." Rick had a general distaste for house pets and particular concerns about Rico. And he was a busy man, working for the local financial investment firm. There was no way he'd waste his lunch break walking even himself. "His mouth was bloody."

"Not Rico."

"Could have been a squirrel. But Brendan, if you don't keep him tied up, I'll get rid of him myself. Sorry," he added in a meeker tone. "But it's like living with a time bomb. We don't need any more trouble."

"Trouble. Right here in River City!" When his stepfather didn't respond, Brendan prompted, "*The Music Man*?" He'd watched it once with his real father, years ago, because there had been nothing else on television. They'd mocked it, but he still cherished the memory because it was one of the few good, clear ones he had of the man.

"I know the reference."

"Dog starts with a D that rhymes with T, and that stands for trouble. Right here!"

"I know this is funny to you, but if you really want to know, it's been a strain on the marriage."

"Rico? A strain?" He almost laughed thinking of Rico as a new strain of the flu, wiping out marriages left and right, but his stepfather's look brought him up short.

"I think you know what I'm talking about. Don't imagine you've forgotten."

No, thought Brendan. *Don't imagine you'll let me.* Instead he said, "Mom quit yoga two months ago."

"Then maybe she'll take up prayer."

Officer Yellowrobe opened a small, black kit that reminded Brendan of pocket-sized tackle boxes meant for storing dry flies. Inside was a tiny brush, miniature of the broom he used to sweep up brittle crusts and limp bits of lettuce, and a black bottle with a twist-off cap, hexagon-shaped, like some elixir from a fantasy movie. The officer unscrewed it with fingers as broad and flat as the rest of him. He showed the contents to Brendan and Dennis, allowing them to examine the pale powder inside as if it were the first stage of a magic trick, the part where he proved everything was on the up and up. "We call it dust," he said. "It's practically invisible when you apply it." By way of demonstration the police officer produced a dollar from a hand-tooled, leather wallet stamped *BILLY*. He swirled the brush in the bottle. He then painted the dollar in brisk strokes, advising Brendan to lay it on thickest over the bills at the top of the pile.

"You should leave the twenties on top if that's what she's been taking. Is it?" He and Dennis looked at Brendan, who shrugged.

"I guess. I don't *know* if she's taken anything."

The two men exchanged a glance. "Look," the officer started in a voice more condescension than kindness. "I've busted my brother three times. My own brother. He got mixed-up with the wrong people and spent a few years in Deer Lodge on drug charges. If I can do that in the name of justice, you can catch the thief that's been robbing these good people."

Brendan contemplated this. There were a lot of reasons one might put away his own brother, few of which were grounded in noble ideals like justice. "I just don't know."

"That's what the dust is for, kid. Brandon, is it? If her hands glow under this black light, she's guilty. Then you know." He handed the dollar to Dennis who gripped it tightly then passed it back. "See?" He passed a black-light wand over Dennis's palm and it glowed like the Milky Way on a really clear night.

"Guess we got our thief," Brendan joked. Officer Yellowrobe stared him into silence then reviewed the plan. Put the cash till on the back of the toilet as always, let the suspect use the restroom if she asks, lock up and walk with her out the main doors of the mall where Officer Yellowrobe himself would be waiting with his magic wand of truth and justice.

"Nine o'clock?" he asked.

Dennis nodded then looked to Brendan. "Do you have any more questions for the detective?"

Does your brother send you Christmas cards? Did he ever? Do you visit him in prison? Would you take his dog if he asked? Do you tell everyone this story? If so, is it to make you into a hero or to try to make us more human? "No, sir."

The officer paused. "Don't think of it as being a snitch, but more a small-time hero to Denny here."

It was a seven-hour shift, the most excruciating he'd had, not because the deli was busy but because it wasn't. Dennis hovered for a couple hours downing cup after cup of diet Dr. Pepper until he was more wired than usual and decided to go home. "I want you to call me as soon as you know something." Between dishing up pizza and soup for mall employees on break, Brendan fixed himself a ham sub. And he dutifully paid for it, watching the till register his employee ID number for a fifty-percent discount. When time expired on a sad slice of mushroom pizza, he added it to the seven unwanted pieces that had accumulated in the freezer, making a whole pizza which he wrapped in cellophane and sealed with a small sticker shaped like a peanut. Surely this re-use, economical as it was, violated health code?

He poured himself a small cup of ice water, careful to use the 12-ounce styrofoam for which he paid a dime, and he'd just filled the sink with hot, soapy water to scrub potato scut from the bottom of the soup kettle when he heard the jangling bell at the front counter. Wiping his hands on pants already stained with ketchup, grease, and pop syrup, he turned the corner and saw green-eyed Charlene leaning on the counter, hands folded under her small, pointed chin, an irresistible smile on her face. His insides bucked like the little car on the slush machine.

"Brendan!" she chirruped. "Meet my friend Stacy." He was surprised to notice someone else there, a tan woman with highlighted hair and small eyes made smaller by dark makeup. She looked bored and full of herself, the type of girl Brendan chased after in high school because everyone believed she was popular. The type of girl he could get easily because Toby thought he was funny, which meant everyone else thought he was too. He nodded at Stacy who raised her thin-plucked eyebrows in response.

"You're coming out with us tonight, aren't you? Cowboy Jack's? Thirsty Thursday specials?" She fiddled with a gold hoop earring while waiting for his response. When he shrugged okay, she counted out change to buy a diet Coke and told her friend they'd meet up at the bar in forty minutes.

Stacy pouted. "What did I come here for then?"

"Go find Rodney or J.J. We'll double-date." Charlene smiled at Brendan again. Her green eyes held him, mesmerizing, and he leaned on the counter to steady himself. Stacy stalked off, twitching an invisible tail, and Charlene took a seat at the table nearest the back, propping her dress boots on another chair. They were dove gray, barely scuffed. He thought they looked soft to the touch.

"Go ahead," she said, sipping her drink. At first he thought she meant he could touch her boots, but she was looking at the mop propped in the corner. "We'll talk while you close."

He couldn't imagine what they'd talk about ("So how about that missing money?"), but he stuck to his routine, spraying the bleach solution on all the counters, filling the mop bucket. Charlene told him she wasn't staying in Great Falls.

"Going back to school?" Brendan remembered she'd attended some small liberal arts college in Washington.

"Nope, Seattle."

"I thought you wanted to be an actress."

"Seattle's got great theater companies. I can always move to Hollywood when I'm ready. And I'm changing my name. Wanna guess?"

He didn't want to guess. He wanted to shut down the register, let her use the bathroom, and let this long day deal its final blow. He mopped under the bridge of her long legs while she tapped the heels of her boots together.

"C'mon. Guess my name."

"Rumpelstiltskin?"

She gave him an amused, appraising look. "Why don't you have a girlfriend?"

"People are afraid of me." He said it without thinking.

"What? Now you're being goofy. You're the sweetest guy!" He wanted to believe she really thought that, but it sounded empty, like something a Stacy would say.

"You never know," he answered, regretting it instantly because instead of sounding mysterious, he sounded pure dork.

Brendan squeezed the dingy water from the mop and watched the clock slide toward nine. He could shut down the till at any time now. Instead he turned to the bright-eyed girl and asked, "Have you ever done something that you had no idea what the consequences would be?"

The slush machine whirred, the Thunderbird dipping and surging in its track, his bosses' faces looping around like lunatic phantoms.

Charlene laughed her lovely laugh. "Who hasn't?"

"Like what?" The grating of metal gates crashing down echoed through the empty mall. She sneaked a peek at her watch. "What have you done?"

"Moving to Seattle."

"You don't know the consequences yet."

"Isn't that what you just asked?"

Brendan shook his head. "I meant something where you've already learned how all the dominos fell."

"I guess nothing all that major," Charlene confessed. She pulled a compact from her bag and applied more plum lipstick. "What about you?"

He looked at her for a long time until she glanced up, her lips still pressed together, smearing the color around. "Nah," he said. "I'm boring."

"I think you're interesting." She offered no supporting evidence, and so he turned the tiny key on the cash register, ran the daily slip for Debbie, who he knew would match it to the cash first thing in the morning, and carried the till to the back, leaving it on top of the toilet as usual. He opened the kit and the bottle, partially plugged the little opening with one finger and shook the dust all over the twenties, easy as seasoning meat.

It had started as a routine autumn Saturday. Early morning weightlifting at the high school, training for football. After, he and Toby went out for donuts and gigantic soda pops. Then, as usual, they cruised around in Toby's shiny, black Ford F150 with the Chevy pee-on decal and the *NO FAT CHICKS* bumper sticker, and his personalized license plate: BUM SKI (SKI BUM, his first choice, was already taken). They'd always shoot the shit, rate the hottest girls at school, argue for or against God's existence, or talk about the ski shop they planned to open after college. Toby's dog, Rico Suave, always came along. He barked at anyone who came within three feet of the vehicle, and Toby liked to joke that he got the dog to protect the truck. Brendan suspected Toby got both to complete some vision of himself as the ideal Montana Man. Tough, expensive truck with a gun rack (empty), a dog that strangers feared, a starting position on the football team and the letter jacket to prove it. His senior portraits featured all of his prizes, and he'd tried to get Brendan to borrow the dog so they'd match. Brendan's mother had said over her dead body would he pose with a dog, gun, or truck. "Why not wear a T-shirt that says *I'm a big, cheating dick?*" she'd asked. There was his long-gone father, still ruining things eleven years later.

That day they had their drinks wedged between their thighs, Rico panting between them, "riding bitch" as Toby liked to say, and they'd just exited the highway, back in city limits, when Toby slowed the truck and asked, "Ever wonder what it would be like to run over a person?"

It wasn't a crazy statement if you had the context of what happened that summer just before school started. At least that's how Brendan tried to explain it before he stopped explaining. There'd been a keg party a few miles out of town at a gravel pit. A couple of drunk sophomore boys had wandered off to pee, and a carload of junior girls driving the highway in search of the party had come around a curve, no time to stop for Mark Whipple who'd been pissing on the yellow center line. The driver convinced herself she'd hit a deer, driving on even as her friends screamed and dialed their mothers on their cell phones instead of 911. There had been a school-wide memorial for Mark on the second day of classes, and the driver, hospitalized with a nervous breakdown, was still fresh fodder for gossip.

Brendan's response was now a frozen mammoth in his mind, a forever-perfect specimen from an era long gone. Tested, measured, every angle examined. He said, "You mean like her?" and pointed to the woman jogging on his side of the road a block ahead. "Fifty points. Twenty more if you leave the sign standing." The woman, in a pale-pink tracksuit, was approaching one of the welcome signs posted on the perimeter of the city: *The Good People of Great Falls Welcome You!*

Every teenager he knew said things like that in a car. Ten points for the guy in the wheelchair, fifteen bonus if you can make him do a wheelie. Things like that.

Toby had said, "Okay," gunning the engine, and Brendan had laughed. The next thing he knew the truck was on the sidewalk against a wall of bushes, their leaves tipped orange and yellow. He always remembered how the leaves seemed like tiny matches just struck, ready to consume whatever they touched. Rico was barking, the sound painfully loud in his ears, his pants were soaked, all cold and sticky, and his nose was bleeding, though he couldn't figure out why.

"What the fuck?" he'd whimpered, wiping his nose along his arm in a sticky red trail. His stomach seemed still to be moving, pressing all directions though the truck was still. The dog kept up his maniacal barking, and Toby stared straight ahead, the strangest expression on his face, something Brendan had fumbled to describe because he'd never seen it before. When the dog settled into a plaintive whine, Brendan heard for the first time a persistent, low moaning. It was coming from somewhere under the truck.

That was the story he'd stopped explaining. Because everyone always asked, aloud or not, what he'd done next. He hadn't even called his mother on his cell phone. All he remembered was petting the frantic dog, telling him it would be okay.

"I'm changing my stage name to Charlemagne," she was saying, her pop cup empty except for the ice which she rattled to a rhythm in her head like she was already two-stepping at The Boot Scoot, spinning on her heel and nodding her head. "He was a king and a sort of patron of the arts. Powerful guy. That's got to be a good luck charm, eh?"

"Sure." His heart was banging off-beat. Most employees were exiting the main entrance or scooting out the delivery doors unseen. "Well, I guess we're done here."

Charlene stood, tossed her cup into the just-emptied trash. "Maybe two words like Charla Main? Or just one like Cher or Madonna? What do you think?"

Brendan said, "Whichever. They're both nice."

She touched his hand. "Hey, could I use the bathroom here real quick? My contacts are bothering me." She blinked her large, green eyes a few times.

"You know where it is."

He stood, waiting. Waved to Allison, the jewelry store manager who liked her gyro without lettuce and Tourney, the limping security officer who had no clue that a crime was happening at that moment. In fact, Debbie and Dennis had left him out of the loop completely, going straight to Great Falls' Finest.

Tourney, always cheerful, called out, "How's it hanging?"

"Low and to the left."

"You watching the game tonight?"

"Sure," Brendan shouted, no clue what he meant, though he guessed baseball. He couldn't recall Tourney's favorite team. In Montana, sporting goods stores carried everybody's jerseys since there were no professional teams. Just the Bobcat-Grizzly collegiate rivalry, and he had no interest in that anymore.

Charlene appeared at his side and casually linked her arm in his. He ached to imagine the date they could have had if he'd been twenty-one. "Ready?" she asked.

"As never."

She giggled and pressed against his hip. Her hair fell over her eyes and there was something so easy and beautiful in the way her hand swept the hair off again that he paused to look at her before snapping off the lights.

"What?"

There was a strange halo of green around one of her irises, like the color was bleeding out. "Your eye. It looks weird."

"Damn contact lens," she mumbled, rolling her eyes up then sliding the lens back into place with her ring finger. He turned off the overhead lights but kept his eyes fixed on her face, now rosy from the glow of the cherry slush machine.

"There's an exit over by the women's restroom," he said. "Goes out to the back lot."

"I don't need the restroom. Everything's back in place." She blinked three times rapidly and smiled.

"No, but you need that exit," he replied, turning toward the main mall entrance and nodding toward the thick figure of Officer Yellowrobe leaning just outside the glass doors, the cherry of his cigarette flaring as he sucked in. Earlier he'd been in jeans and a jacket. Now he wore his uniform.

Charlene followed his gaze. Her eyes widened as she turned back and drew away from his side. She searched his face then said in a clear, cold voice, "She takes money from the till all the time, Brendan."

"Who?"

"Debbie. Gets her nails done, buys a sweater on sale. Just punches No Sale and takes what she wants. I've even seen her pocket the five bucks from those crappy, leftover pizzas." The mall grew dimmer as more managers turned off overhead lights.

"But she's co-owner. It's hers."

Charlene shook her head and coughed up a shallow laugh. "Come on. It belongs to the business. Money comes up missing—that's what they told you I bet—and they pin it on an employee, write it off on their taxes." Her eyes in the low light were hazel, not that brilliant, convincing green, and he suddenly realized that she must wear tinted contacts. "They wanted me to help catch a thief too, Brendan. Some high-school girl who quit before you were hired."

"Did you?" His heart continued to bang around in his chest, tight and erratic.

"Did I *what?*" She stared at him, unwavering.

But he couldn't ask again. He pointed down the short hall to the women's restroom and made a shooing gesture. Charlene paused, blew him a kiss, and called, "A girlfriend, Brendan. Get one!" Then she two-stepped her way into the shadows.

"Where is she?" Officer Yellowrobe scanned the parking lot, stubbed out his cigarette and dropped it in the butt-filled ashtray beside him.

Brendan shrugged. "Didn't show."

"You were talking to someone."

"Girl I knew from high school. She just wanted my buddy's phone number." The lies came easily, but he felt a sheen of sweat cooling his upper lip.

"You got my dust kit?"

"No. I left it in Dennis's office like you said." He shivered as the wind swirled into the sheltered cubby of the entrance.

"Can I give you some advice?" The officer fumbled in his pocket for another cigarette which he didn't light but held in the air like a piece of chalk, a teacher making a point.

"Didn't stop you before. Officer."

Officer Yellowrobe stared at him until Brendan had to look away, feigning sudden interest in the motorcycle that zipped past them. Eddie from the Foot Locker. Bought a resell pizza for five dollars every Friday night.

"The world is full of charming no-goods. You think their shine will rub off on you until you discover it's really a spotlight pinning you to the fence."

"O-kay. Is that a metaphor or an anecdote? I've blocked out twelfth-grade English."

At that Officer Yellowrobe laughed, and Brendan nearly returned his grin before the policeman added, "You're so lucky that woman didn't die. You'd have been named in a lawsuit, buddy, maybe charged with a crime."

"I didn't do anything," Brendan whispered.

"Seems to be a real talent of yours."

His mother was on the floor in front of a late-night comedy show. She appeared to be bowing, worshipping the host. He realized it was a classic yoga pose, downward dog, followed by resting child or something like that. His mother's legs were tucked under her body, arms up and out, face hidden like when they had to put their heads down on their desks in elementary school. The teacher would bark, "Heads down," and they'd all cross their arms and bury their faces. He couldn't remember why. It wasn't a safety drill, and he thought maybe the lights were turned off like it was a resting period. Or was it a class-wide punishment? If so, he remembered no shame, just the comfort of shutting out the world and breathing in the orange-scented oil they used to buff the battered wooden desks.

"Hey," he said to the woman collapsed at his feet.

She peeked out through the gap in her armpit and said a muffled hello. She already sounded calmer than she had for the last few months, and she hadn't brought out the wine yet. Slowly his mother unwound her limbs and pushed up from the floor. "Practice," she said.

"Anybody call for me?"

"No." She dragged the word out a couple syllables, curious, but he merely shrugged. Maybe his boss didn't care. And even if Charlene had his number, he suspected she was having too much fun boot-scooting and leaving a trail of invisible fairy dust every time she bought a round. He looked down at the index finger he'd used to partially plug the neck of the bottle of dust, imagined how his fingerprint would pulse with silver light under that black-light wand.

"Is Rick off praying?"

"Brendan. Be nice." He assumed they'd had a fight and some sort of reconciliation while he was at work. The shifting allegiances always confused him.

"Who's that church person anyway?" he asked. He pressed his finger into the fabric of the sofa. Peered at the indent. No visible fairy dust.

"Who?"

"You said someone went to the church where Rick prays."

"Laura Dermott?"

"That sounds right." He tried to remember what else that finger had touched. Particles of dust everywhere, invisible sparkles.

"She's one of the whores your dad went after. Your *real* dad."

Brendan whistled. "Wow, Mom. That was years ago. You need to let some things go."

His mother squeezed her eyes tight like a spotlight had flooded her face with light. "And maybe you let too much go."

"You're sure no one called?" He could imagine Dennis as the type to appeal to a mother. *I'm sorry to bother you, ma'am, but your son is in grave moral danger…*

"No one called. Why? What's going on?" He watched his mother press at her eyes with the heel of one hand and realized it was only her contact lenses bothering her again. She was too vain to take them out before bed, said her glasses made her look like a housefly. He wondered why anyone would wear contacts if all they did was hurt.

"There was this girl," Brendan said. "She invited me out after work."

"Really?" His mother's voice was airy with hope. "She's pretty?"

"Really pretty."

"You've got to watch out for those ones," his mother said, shaking her head, but she was smiling. Suddenly, she curled her finger, beckoning. "You've got to see this."

She led him to his stepfather's study where Rick was asleep, head tilted back in his chair at an angle that looked painful. And there, a few feet away, lay Rico, snoring and drooling. "Hey, Down Dog," Brendan whispered. The dog stirred, raised its head, and fell back with a grunt and a fart.

"I didn't know Rick let him in the house."

"Me neither." His mother had a peculiar smile on her face, tender like she'd caught an overly cute toddler being naughty. "They seem to like each other despite it all."

He didn't know whether to feel envy or relief. Rico had narrowly escaped Animal Control right after The Incident. A witness claimed the dog had gone after the helpless jogger when Brendan opened the door. The detective in the little room cited some statistic that Rottweilers were three times more likely to kill humans than pitbulls.

"Nobody was killed," Brendan insisted.

"You think that makes it okay."

"No." He would always see that crumpled pink shape under the truck, hear the bewildered shrieks as she tried to kick the dog with her free foot, the other held fast in Rico's jaws as he tried to drag her out.

"According to neighbors, Toby was training that animal to attack," the detective suggested. Ridiculous. Brendan had never wavered on this point, knowing it would seal Toby and Rico's fates.

"The dog was trying to save her. He was pulling her away from the truck."

The detective had laughed. He'd actually laughed at Brendan. "And what were you doing?" he asked then.

"I didn't do anything!"

"I know," the detective said. "So…you're free to go." And somehow, he'd felt no relief.

Brendan watched the dog's ribs shudder with each snore then followed his mother back to the living room. He slumped in the recliner, and she sat cross-legged on the floor, back straight. He was tired, but he couldn't imagine sleep. A few miles away, that really pretty girl was stamping her boots to honky-tonk, sloshing beers bought on someone else's dime. He imagined her smiling coyly at a man who wasn't Brendan, ready to head into the sunset far from Great Falls. Maybe she'd change her name, change her eye color, change her luck.

"What happens if I lose my job?"

He braced himself for a tongue-lashing, certain he'd re-awaken his mother's long-held suspicions that he was no good, a replica of his genetic father. Instead, she changed the channel to local news, inhaled long and deep, rounded then dropped her shoulders. She said, "You'll just find another one. You've got to pay your way somehow."

He nodded, and they both studied the small screen where the weatherman prepared his forecast, arms spread wide over a map of their region, a small clicker hidden in his palm, ready to change the map.

HIGH ON THE DIVIDE

The men are descended from hard-rock miners, their lungs gone to granite, their hearts chunks of ore. "On the rocks," they say when they order their bourbon. The bar is O'Sullivan's. The city is Butte. They call me Angel of Mercy because they're Catholic and can never remember my name, not when their eyes mist with memory. Not when they cry. You can cry at O'Sullivan's. In a city where the Bulldogs are Double-A wrestling champs year after year and the jail fills on St. Paddy's by noon, there are still places where grown men can cry.

I refill their glasses and leave extra napkins, and they whisper, "You're the Angel of Mercy. Sent by the Lord." Sometimes, when it's someone with a sense of humor—Dylan Downey or Old Man McClure—I say, "I was hired by Liam, and he's not the Lord."

"Yes, Angel, we know that. But who will tell Liam and break his old heart?"

"You can't break his heart," says another. "It's stone."

And they all fall to silence, labored breathing, alcoholic fumes I could light. Sometimes I imagine flicking a lighter and blasting another hole in this scarred mountain. New veins to explore, new work for this town.

The men, when they're sober, say go back to school. "Girl, that's the future. A college degree." And though none of their wives—first, second, or third—had degrees, they want more for me, this future whose fingers they can touch.

When they're drunk, they say, "Angel. Don't leave. Take us into the next world. Angel. Mercy."

I've nowhere to go, so I stay their saint, serving up spirits, mopping those broken circles they leave under their drinks. Sometimes I imagine flicking that lighter and starting to smoke. My pink lungs will seize up, and I'll cough when I need to inhale. Sometimes I touch my wrist to remember the pulse. Michael Rourke sobbed one night—a sound like choking—because he couldn't find his pulse. He wept that he'd died and, since that one pope erased purgatory, he was surely in hell.

"So I'm a demon, am I, Mikey?"

"Mercy, no," he said when he could breathe again. "I know I'm in hell because I can't touch you. You're miles away, up in the sky, holding Our Lord's punctured hand."

I clutched his thin wrist, pressed his finger to the groove below his thumb, and I counted with him. *One, two, three, four. You're not pounding on death's door.*

That night Liam couldn't drive him, so I walked him home, counting his heartbeats aloud on the steep mountain streets. *One, two, three, four, Mikey's heart ain't made of ore.*

"Unless it's gold," he whispered, stumbling at the threshold of his small, dark house. I wavered there in the doorway, unsure. Tuck him in? But I wasn't his mother, and I wasn't a saint. I shut the door on his cave, sealing him in. *Fool's gold,* I thought I heard him say, but the door was metal and warped and it could have been *whose gold* or *too cold* or so many other things.

One night the cowboy comes in, and I feel for my pulse. Thumping, thumping for escape. I think of that lighter under the bar, this place sky-high in a shower of flame, my blood rushing out of me, my heart set free. I crouch low to the bar, swish my hair in my face, and Danny Riordan says, "Angel, you okay?" And one by one, these men still on their bourbons but ready for Coke walk to me. Wobbly as toddlers. "Is she sick?" "Is she hiding?" "Is her heart broke?"

Silence. Then someone, not me, says, "An angel's heart can't break."

And someone else, the cowboy, says, "No, it just flies away."

No one here entertains strangers, so none of them like how he steps through their words. They grumble as if they are young men with strong hearts, strong lungs, strong fists.

No stranger to me, this cowboy. He'd held to my finger a circle so perfect that I fled all my dreams of riding over the plains into the setting sun. I came back to this place high on the Divide where whole generations believe the sun is lit on the end of a wick a mile underground.

The men cluster tight like they can save me. But they're the ones drowning in bourbon and rum, in memory shafts they've cut with too little air.

"You could cry here," I say. "You could pour out a bottle and, depending on which side of this mountain you chose, it might join the Pacific. Or head to the Gulf."

The cowboy knows. He studies the men, how they clutch their drinks and stare. Later, he will say *stony stares*.

That night I think of gold. Golden rings, golden plains, his bare golden arms, those golden sunsets melting through our golden years.

I let the lighter decide. Flame on the first try means "yes." And it lights like a tiny sun. I inhale this air soaked with bourbon and the sour breath of old men. Nothing explodes. I flick the lighter again, and it glows in the dark bar. Circles of light on every man's glass. Extinguished as soon as I raise my thumb.

I flick it again and again, but that night the lighter is constant. The cowboy waits just beyond the glow.

So I leave these men descended from miners. Without mercy. I unlace my angel wings, reckless as I abandon what they know of copper, what they've taught me of gold. Broken rock, all that broken rock.

WALK WITH THE
ANIMALS

Carson was older, just shy of forty, and he'd lived in places that seemed exotic to us then—Bangladesh, Vancouver, Idaho. He claimed that Georgia-Pacific had sent him to Crossett, Arkansas, just to tutor us kids about the world, and instead of feeling the insult there, we swallowed his attentions whole, even held our mouths open for more. We were barely in our twenties, and all of us had lived our whole lives in southeast Arkansas. "Christ," laughed Carson when we told him that. "I've traveled through southeast *Asia*!"

Benny had tried to leave. He started at a small university thirty miles away, but after his pledge brothers beat him so bad his kidneys failed and he lost a week of memories to the intensive care unit in Pine Bluff, his mother had withdrawn him, threatening to sue everyone involved, including a doctor she'd noticed taking a smoke break while her son was in a coma. "He was filling his lungs with poison while my baby struggled to wake up and see his mama's face!" she'd rage to anyone who would listen.

Benny said it sure wasn't her face he wanted to see first. In fact, he wanted to see his fraternity brothers, to be sure they weren't mad at him for being the only one to pass out.

"They were just tryin' to beat the queer out of me, Sharon," he explained when he was recovered and back in Crossett, angry now that he'd never be a full-fledged brother. "But I'll pay fancy doctors to have it taken out when Mama gets that fat ole settlement. Then you and me'll get married," he teased in his favorite hick accent. I smiled at him, wondering if his "brothers" had learned something or only guessed what Benny still wouldn't tell me straight. Or maybe that was initiation, someone beating you into a whole new you of their choosing.

Ginger and I had never gone anywhere after graduating high school. I'd talked about beauty school for a while, until my daddy said, "Girl, you ain't messin' your hands in no black girls' ratty hair. So think again."

When I repeated that to Carson one night while we were all hanging out at his place, he let me practice braiding his long, graying hair to see if I was any good. As I worked my fingers over his scalp, he moaned a little and said I had good hands. Giving hands. He said my daddy was wrong to not let me go to beauty school. Then he told me stories about lynchings and civil-rights demonstrations, things I'd never studied in my classes at school. When I said how sorry I felt for those folk, he told me that only someone who thinks he's as good as God can feel sorry for somebody else. "'Feel sorry for' shouldn't be in your vocabulary. *Empathize*," he said. Then, as an afterthought, "Just not too much."

Ginger held up the only photo in the room, a snapshot of a middle-aged woman in a bathing suit, one hand shading her eyes. "Who's this?"

Carson stared at it a long moment before saying, "My mother." He shook his hair loose from my braid and added, "I keep it there to remind me to *empathize*."

The photo was gone the next time we visited. I checked that word in Benny's good-as-new college dictionary, and for a week I looked in people's eyes and imagined I felt my heart going right out of me and into them. I felt Miss Ann's sick, sharp loneliness since her husband rolled his ATV and snapped his spine. I truly felt my daddy's shame and anger at the people who called him about his credit cards. Worse, I felt how the black folk that I served at the diner hated me. Carson said I was projecting and not empathizing. He said the fact is they didn't think twice about me and I might as well accept that most of the world felt the same.

"You just suffer when you want people to love you," he said. "You could learn a thing or two about detachment." But that's what I felt before I quit trying to feel other people's feelings. Cold, uncooked hate served up as disinterest.

Ginger was the most susceptible to Carson, the first to fall into him. While Benny had his mother and I had my daddy to blame for our stalled lives, she was on her own. Her parents had suffocated in a trailer fire that the town still rumored was started by the teenaged Ginger herself. I'd seen her the day after the tragedy and she'd been out of her head with grief. Still, people will talk. She'd been a wild child, but the deaths quickly sucked the wild away. She lived in her own small house out toward the wildlife refuge where she could hear the ducks crying, and with her father's life-insurance payout she bought reefer by the quart-size bag from a contact that she refused to divulge. She said if we discovered him, she'd cut us off. The pot kept her calm, kept all of us even keel and never too worried about anything. We didn't pry.

One day, after Ginger bought her usual somewhere behind the cougar cage at the small, pathetic Crossett Zoo, Carson had stopped her. That's how they met. He'd set a heavy hand on her shoulder from behind. She thought he was an undercover cop, and as she tells it, she nearly ran straight toward the starving cougar than risk jail, but he grabbed her arm tight and said he only wanted a dime bag and some conversation. The spring sky split into rain, and they smuggled into a shed with the potbelly pigs and got high so the smell wouldn't bother them. "Girl, you shoulda seen those blobby-backed pigs with their eyes rolled back," she told me that night. "Imagine what they do when they get the munchies!"

"How did this guy know you had weed?" I finally asked after we'd smoked ourselves silly waiting for Benny to get off work from the local poultry farm where he gathered dead chickens in a wheelbarrow and cleaned up shit.

"He spends a lot of time at the zoo. Talks to the animals like that Dr. Doolittle." She giggled. "Said he'd seen me waiting there over the months and figured it out."

"You better pick a new place," I cautioned, "or you'll have your own cage."

So Carson became a part of our smoking circle, and Ginger admired him like a guardian angel, giving him dope for free even though he made enormous amounts of money at GP. What work he did or where his paychecks went, we didn't know. He lived in a modest house near downtown, drove a car that was ten years old, and dressed in clothes that looked to be from a discount table or the Goodwill. Decent but never quite right. Benny speculated that Carson was a millionaire just looking for worthy people to surprise with enormous wads of cash. The idea took with us and one night while Carson was working we smoked a bowl and shared what we'd do with that money. Benny wanted a nice car and a condo in Little Rock, far from the smell of poultry.

"Dream bigger," I advised. "Little Rock is not the top of the world."

He shrugged and said he wanted to stay near his mama.

"Mama's boy," I challenged, feeling a sting of meanness under my buzz. I opened a beer, hoping to numb whatever demon was after me. I liked Benny, more than most anyone. That's why I found it easy to torture him.

"Why? Where would you go, Miss Hoity-Toity? Memphis?"

I thought about that, and shook my head no. Buildings were nothing special, however many, however tall. I would want more trees, more forest like all over Arkansas, only I wouldn't want to know a single gossiping soul.

"Idaho," I said. "That's where I'd go."

"Oh hell, what kind of crush do you have on Carson? Idaho!" He expelled a sudden puff of breath in disgust. Ginger put away her pipe and opened a beer for her and one for Benny. She turned to me.

"Do you?"

"Do I what?"

"Have a crush on Carson." She sipped her beer slowly, keeping her eyes on my face.

"No, but I think Benny does." I'd noticed how he laughed at every stupid thing Carson said, how his long lashes lowered coquettishly when Carson glanced at him. I could almost imagine how his vision was blurred that way, enough to smear the details of disinterest, annoyance even, from his object's expression. Ginger and I both knew that Carson only tolerated Benny and would rather be alone with us. He'd once said, "That kid doesn't get things, girls. He's not as smart as you two. Not as fun to talk to. And he always smells of chicken shit." We'd nodded solemnly as if every word were true.

"Bullshit!" Benny shouted at me, his voice wavering so I could see it snaking out at me, fangless and still trying to strike. "He's a fake, and he's old. And a guy, Sharon. He's a *guy*." Too many chemicals, I thought, still watching the outline of his voice.

"I just don't want to see you hurt," I said, shrugging, turning to leave.

Ginger stopped me at my car. I could still hear Benny raging, only now he was screaming that *I* was bullshit. "Hey, don't go. He'll get over it. You know better than to go after a guy's manhood like that."

I'd dug my fingers right into the wound. I knew that, and I wasn't apologizing.

"No, I'm going. I feel funky and Daddy Dearest might already be back." He'd driven a rig full of tomatoes to Memphis. Full-time work this time of year. He'd be in a good mood that would sour quickly if I wasn't there to greet him.

She nodded and closed the car door for me. A dull crash sounded from her kitchen. "I'll get rid of Angry Pants."

"Hold on. You never told what you'd do with Carson's money."

"I don't think he's any millionaire." She fumbled in her pocket for her cigarettes.

"Just play along. What would you do? Where would you move to?"

Ginger looked up into the black starry night and said, "I'd stay right here."

"You'd stay here with these *assholes* who think you killed your parents?" I was suddenly angry for her. I believed I was *empathizing.*

She shrugged and lit a cigarette. "I'd buy up all the land around here, everything not owned by GP or the railroad, and I'd donate it to the refuge. More alligators, more black bears, more deer and ducks that these assholes couldn't shoot. I'd make this place sacred again."

It sounded like something Carson would say, and it smelled of what Benny would call bullshit.

"Walk with the animals, talk with the animals. Maybe I'll go to Memphis after all," I said, starting the engine. "Or further." Once I'd backed out onto the highway, I looked over to where she stood. The smoke from her cigarette snaked like Benny's voice, wrapping around the porch light on its way to heaven.

Sometimes Benny and I fought that way because we had no one else to fight with. We were still too dependent on our parents, we weren't thugs like a lot of kids who threw their anger in rocks and bullets at rival gangs, and Ginger's tragedy made her off-limits. But we had grown up in Crossett together, and after weeks of scooping dead chickens or serving dead chickens, one of us would explode, usually Benny.

After our last argument about him wanting to rush a fraternity, he'd picked me up and taken me on a long walk through the wildlife refuge. I kept my eyes ahead on the forest, knowing a few bears lived there. I wanted to glimpse them shredding a pine or rooting for grubs, something they couldn't do in the concrete bear cage at the zoo. I wanted to be a little afraid. No bars, no wire fences.

Benny said as we walked, "I think you're jealous. You just don't want me to be part of anything."

"You're a part of something already."

"What?"

"Crossett, Arkansas. It's in your blood."

"Then find a vampire to suck it all out." He leapt suddenly, rolling me to the ground where he bit at my neck. I laughed and slapped him at the same time. Dry leaves and dirt in my hair, small welt on my throat. I shook my head, threatened to tell my boyfriend.

"He's not your boyfriend."

"We've been seeing each other." He was a guy from the college, someone who worked at Georgia-Pacific the summer before Benny started his semester. He'd come into the restaurant after a shift, and we'd started by talking, then went for long drives that ended up hot and heavy down in the wetlands. He kept promising to take me to Memphis.

"Not exclusively." So quiet I almost didn't hear him.

"What?"

"He's in the fraternity, Sharon. He gets around. Trust me on that."

We were silent for several moments, moments full of bird calls and wind-crackled pines and my sniffles.

"You don't want me to be part of anything either." That's all I said, but he curled his arm around my shoulder, and we stood quietly under the canopy of trees a long time, until the dark crept in.

This time there were no walks. Benny hadn't spoken to me in almost two weeks, our longest stretch yet, when Ginger announced she wanted to have a dinner party. I'd never heard her describe any of our gatherings that way, but she said it was time we classed up our act and tried something besides potato chips and pot.

"Dress up," she said on the phone. "Just a little."

The only skirt I owned was the one I had to wear at the diner, and it was stained with gravy drippings and dribbled coffee. I settled for a pair of black pants that I wore on those rare occasions when we'd go to the bars in Monroe, Louisiana. In the back of my closet, I found a ruffled blouse of my mother's, red with a low elastic collar that showed a scoop of skin on my throat and my back. I pulled the pins from my hair, pleased to see the tiny curls spraying perfectly around my face and throat like dark tendrils of ivy.

When I came into the kitchen, my father stopped stirring his tomato soup and stared, his expression uncertain. Finally he said, "That was your mama's shirt."

I nodded, knowing he didn't like talking about her. She'd run away to Pensacola with another man. Benny's biological father. That had been years ago, and they hadn't stayed together long, both of them serial lovers, notorious for having dated nearly everyone in Crossett, single or married, who wasn't fixed fast to a church's morals. Now they were working on all of Florida, near as I could tell. She called me sometimes when she thought she was getting married again. She'd asked me to be her maid of honor three separate times, and I still hadn't seen Florida.

"You're not wearing it right." He set down the spoon on the stovetop where it left a bloody smear and pulled the stretchy collar down off my shoulders.

"But my bra straps are showing now."

He looked perplexed and somewhat embarrassed by the black bands cutting across my shoulders, and then he turned back to the stove. "I guess you better wear it back up then."

But I left it that way, bra exposed, as I drove to Ginger's, only covering my shoulders again when I saw Carson's beater in the driveway. Benny's truck was not there.

The kitchen smelled sweet with thick, fried fat, and I was surprised to see what looked like a duck in the oven.

"It *is* a duck in the oven," Ginger explained, re-tying the apron that covered her short, flower-print dress. "We've been preparing it since this morning, haven't we?" She turned to smile at Carson, who was sipping a Coke. When he smiled back, I realized that they'd slept together, and I instinctively backed away and got myself a Coke too, trying to absorb that.

"Sure you don't want a beer or a shot of something?" Carson asked. "We've got some sort of bourbon."

"I'll have what you're having," I replied, and he grinned then, a slow-spreading, toothy grin. The Cheshire cat or some cartoon predator. "Where's Benny anyway?"

The two of them exchanged quick glances, and Ginger answered. "Oh, we didn't invite him. I don't think he likes duck."

"You don't like duck," I pointed out. "Not shot down for eating, you don't."

"We didn't shoot it," she answered, not meeting my eyes. "Carson found it."

"We're eating *found* duck?" The only place you could find duck this time of year was at the local zoo, though wood ducks lived in the refuge year-round. I tried not to think of this.

"At a supermarket, Sharon," Carson said in a soothing voice. "The gourmet mart." Thanks to all the diverse non-Southerners Georgia-Pacific brought in, Crossett had a few treasures for its size, including the gourmet mart and a massage/aromatherapy parlor that was rumored to double as what is politely called an escort service. Never mind that there is nowhere to be escorted to in Crossett, Arkansas.

"I just wanted to give you both a little more culture, and I couldn't find any filet mignon," Carson continued.

"Duck is culture, huh? Just wait until fall. The bed of every four-by-four in town will be full of culture. High society in L.A. That's short for Lower Arkansas," I added smugly.

"You'll like the way I do it," he said, fixing his eyes on mine until I looked away. I finished my Coke quickly because I hate when it gets warm and syrupy, and I wandered around Ginger's little house studying everything for clues to whatever it was I sensed had changed in her. But everything looked the same, from the cheap Monet prints to the stacks of well-thumbed Stephen King books that she read alone late at night to scare herself. Ginger liked to imagine rabid bears or psychotic drifters creeping up to her window from the backside of the refuge. She called me once when her imagination overpowered her rational mind. I'd driven over to find every light in the house burning, crawled into the double bed, and whispered secrets until she fell asleep. Then I'd slipped home again, wondering in the morning if it was all a dream.

"The duck will be a while longer," Ginger announced, pushing a tray of crackers and funny-smelling cheese my way. "I'm going to roll a fattie." She took off her apron and bounced into the back room, her deliberate ass-shaking not unnoticed by Carson who then turned and told me my hair was unusually pretty tonight.

I blushed again. He'd found a weakness, and he pressed his point further by saying, "It's a shame you haven't gone to beauty school." I shrugged and pulled up the sleeve slipping off my shoulder.

Ginger returned with a joint big enough for six people and, after ceremoniously lighting it with her Elvis Presley lighter, she gave me the first drag. I knew something was going to happen that night. I felt it like an electric hum in the air, like an inevitable storm approaching. You can batten down the hatches and pray for safety or let the winds and rains pummel you while you pray to be strong. I pulled hard on the joint, and held the sweet smoke in my lungs until I imagined it was the smoke of a shot and scorched duck. I let it all out with the cough of a novice.

They laughed, and we smoked until we were hazy and the kitchen timer had long since burst its shrill ring. I remember we dined on the duck because I was fascinated with how Carson's long fingers pulled every dark web of meat from the bones. I don't much remember the taste. I think it was gamey, but that's what everyone says about wild animals. There was mango sauce and green beans. Then pecan pie with chocolate sauce because as Carson said, "Chocolate's an aphrodisiac."

Ginger lit candles when the natural light started to fade, and Carson lit another joint from a wick. I passed on the hit, already feeling dangerously light and unreal, and as I strained to hear night owls mooning over the refuge, I felt strangely out of balance. They were touching in the shadows where they thought I couldn't see, Benny wasn't with us, and no one was saying anything smart or insightful like all the times before.

I cleared my throat and asked in a hoarse voice, "Carson, what's the sound of one hand clapping?"

"That's a koan," he said. "You don't get to know the answer until you're enlightened." I noticed his one hand cupping Ginger's ass.

"Enlighten me."

He grinned again and handed me the joint. "Just inhale."

I did, and I soon regretted it, because I felt that part of me was on the floor, part of me scraping the ceiling like a helium balloon. Sharon on the Floor was firmly planted, tugging on an invisible string attached to Sharon on the Ceiling. Sharon on the Ceiling was blindly bobbling, looking for an escape route so she could keep soaring into the stratosphere. All the tugging and bobbling was making me sick.

I felt Carson's hand on my neck, pushing down so the sleeve of my mother's blouse slipped over my shoulder. At the same time, I saw his other hand stroking Ginger's leg all the way up where it disappeared under her hem.

"Where's Benny? You didn't kill him, did you?" As soon as I said it, I believed it, imagining they'd fed him to the starving cougar or those potbelly pigs that ate anything.

They both stared at me and started to laugh. "She's had enough," Ginger giggled.

"Yes, darling," Carson whispered, his hot tongue flicking my ear. "And you gobbled him up at dinner. Roast Benny." He made

a growling sound and bit at my exposed shoulder. I jumped back
and stared from him to Ginger until she put her hand on mine
and told me he was only joking. She stroked my hand and I calmed
down. Sharon on the Floor was wishing I hadn't smoked so much.
Then I felt another hand touching my breast.

I rose up as if to shake that hand off, but Ginger whispered,
"It's okay," and I let him stroke me as tiny bumps rose all
over my skin. Miniature mountain landscape rubbed into
creation by a mortal god, stretching for the sky. Sharon on
the Floor trying to become Sharon on the Ceiling. But was he
rubbing me away like an eraser?

I let myself disappear under his hands.

"Now kiss her," I heard the low, soft voice before Ginger
leaned over and pressed dry lips to my eyebrows. Ticklish,
like when a spider skitters over you. "On the lips." Carson
unzipped my jeans and slid his hand into my panties, old ones
with holes that I only wore because that boyfriend had
disappeared after I asked him about Benny and the hospital.

Ginger tested her lips against mine, but I could feel her
resistance, her wish only to please someone else. She wasn't
even a part of that kiss, so I began kissing her back and she
pulled away, looking to Carson for suggestions. *Be a big girl,
Ginger,* I thought. *It's what you wanted, isn't it? Someone
thinking you were a bigger girl than you really are. Pay up.*

I wanted to empathize with her, but she was a coward at
heart, and that's nothing I wanted to feel. She was never leaving
Crossett or her steady supply of pot. I was, as they say,
becoming enlightened.

Then Carson's lips took over, covering mine in a warm,
wet suck that tasted of grass. I explored his mouth right back,
probing tongue, insistent lips. I wanted to show him he'd
picked the wrong girl. But when I felt his finger like a hook
inside me, all the soft melting of the moment froze. I gasped
aloud. Both Sharons now on the floor, pinned there.

A single moment of suspension, everyone hanging on some
sort of precipice, me believing the next motion could gut me

like a duck, turn me inside out and leave my rawest parts exposed. Then Ginger pulled roughly at his hands. "That's not what you said! You said kissing, only kissing!" She fled to her bedroom, sobbing, stumbling blindly against walls so the pictures shuddered.

I looked up at Carson from where I lay on the floor, my insides still painfully tensed to the finger that was no longer there. The candlelight flickered behind him, flame dancing beyond his hair, his face expressionless, a cutout against the light. He paused, kissed me quickly on the forehead, and sprang to his feet to follow her. I was left alone on the hard wood of the living-room floor, wondering how far I would have gone, whether I would have let him pull me right out of myself.

I zipped my pants, slipped on my sandals, and pressed a hand to my hair where all the pretty pin curls had unrolled into limp strands. Streamers after the party. They were arguing in the dark of the bedroom, her voice high and strangled, his a low, rumbling murmur, soothing as a river at night. Beckoning. I walked toward the closed door to listen better and caught a glimpse of myself in the hall mirror.

In the low lighting, I saw the mid-length dark hair matted around a pale face, eyeliner creased into the sunken spaces below the eyes, and that bright red shirt askew on my shoulders. By candlelight, it was the color of blood already drying. I saw my mother in that mirror, a woman trying to return from the dead, which is always a messy business when you're still alive.

Baby, she whispered to me from inside the mirror. *I'll fly you out to see me real soon. Only I got some things to take care of right now. But, Baby, you just wait—it's gonna be great.*

I whirled around then, walking out the front door into the thick, humid night. Crickets and frogs sawed their songs through the dark, and from the refuge I heard a lonely hooting owl. Calling me, I thought, and I started in that direction, thinking that if I just walked I'd eventually be in a protected space, thinking that since there were no fences or roads holding it in, I'd somehow know when I was safe.

But then I heard the owl again and something like a pained screech, and both seemed to come from the other direction, from town, from the zoo, echoing off concrete floors and rusted bars.

I went to my car, grateful for my foolish habit of leaving the keys in the ignition, unable to imagine walking back into that dark, smoky house. I started the engine and backed up, pretending I didn't see Ginger waving wildly at me from her porch, a backlit puppet figure. Still high, I drove too slowly to Benny's house and parked a block away so I wouldn't wake his mother. I crept to his window and tapped gently. Then harder, whispering his name, hoping he, and not his mother, would hear me over the hum of the air conditioner. Nothing.

Finally, as I stood sweating in the August night, I decided to jimmy the window like we'd done in high school when he was past curfew. Suddenly desperate to see him, I worked the frame with a sharp rock, looking to find the bottom latch I remembered, and sure enough, I cracked the latch and slid the window up. As I wrapped my hands over the ledge to hoist myself up and in, I felt a tug then a sudden, sharp pain in my right hand. Splintered wood, maybe a nail.

Warm blood dribbled between my fingers and I suckled, trying not to touch anything with that messy hand, which made getting inside the room difficult. Still I persisted, struggling and wriggling my way through the small opening, stopping occasionally to suck at my wound, before landing— painfully—on a thin rag rug beside his dresser.

He wasn't there. Later I would discover that he'd been two and half hours away, at a bar in Little Rock, dancing with strange men who soon became familiar. In a few short months he would follow one of those men to Memphis and, eventually, New York City. Then he wouldn't come back, not even at Christmas, and I'd send him the same trinkets I sent my mother, wrapped in the same shiny paper, and I'd foolishly wait for a phone call or three lines on a post card telling me that somewhere in a world I'd never seen someone loved me or, at the very least, felt sorry for me.

But that night Benny's bed was still in Arkansas, neatly made, topped with a quilt his mother had sewn. A stack of compact discs leaned against the pillow. I couldn't read the titles in the dark, but I imagined they were songs he listened to at night to soothe him to sleep. One might have been the Delta blues album I'd bought him when he was unconscious and on dialysis.

Some of his fraternity brothers visited on the first day he was conscious. They brought him a six-pack of root beer and a get-well card inked with strange symbols. "It means 'keep the peace,'" he told me later that day. When I nodded, obviously not understanding, he clarified, "Keep your mouth shut." Some other scared pledge squealed about the ritual beatings to the police detective, but Benny's tires were slashed, and trucks bearing the decals and letters of his former brothers sometimes tailed him closely then sped past, beer bottles crashing against his windshield. He never said anything, just pulled over to check the damage, then pulled back on the road, turning the radio so loud we couldn't talk.

I moved the discs, setting them carefully on the floor, and rolled back the quilt, slipping underneath, curling into myself to protect my hand. That was how Benny found me, dead to the world, a blossom of blood spreading from under the pillow.

He says he stifled a scream and checked my pulse and whispered my name a dozen times. I don't remember that. I just remember him holding my injured hand and asking what happened. His fingers probed the tender, swollen flesh around the puncture and fresh blood oozed from beneath the clot and trickled down the long lifeline creasing my palm.

I looked into his dark, serious eyes and cringed to see myself there, a crumpled girl staining someone else's bedsheets. I held my hand up and thought only of Carson telling me I had good hands. Giving hands. Finally, carefully pressing my bloodied palm against Benny's pale one and curling my fingers around his, I whispered, "It doesn't hurt much." But he flinched first because he knew that it would.

BAIT

I leave a note in the morning-cooled cabin, on the table's yellow oilcloth, a note held neatly under a box of cards from last night's disastrous game of rummy. *Took the children on a hike in the wild. Love Me.* I almost place a comma after "love" but leave the command, resisting the question mark my pen wants to add.

The sun strums the golden meadow where the girls chase each other with dead pine branches, their squeals pitched unnervingly high like a hare in its last unclawed moment. Libby and Anna, ages seven and five, "angels" according to my friends whose own flesh-and-blood offspring refuse taming. They tell me I am lucky, that I'm doing a wonderful job with these girls who aren't even mine, and the only one to refute the glory of my success is their father.

"You still don't understand what it means to be a mother," he says, frustrated when I mention marriage and cruelly wonder aloud if I should just move on. "It's more than ice cream and a matinee every other weekend." Even here he chastises me for letting Anna pee in a bucket. "Give her the flashlight and make her go outside. I don't want them to be babies."

I call to the girls, tell them to use the outhouse one more time, and they scramble obediently to the freestanding closet where wasps nest in the eaves and spiders web the toilet-paper holder over and over. I finish lacing my boots.

"Ready?" They're standing before me with branches for walking sticks.

"Is Daddy coming?" asks Anna, and I shake my head no, reminding them that he is fishing, that lunch will be a nice rainbow trout if we're lucky. Libby makes a soft yum sound while her sister frowns and insists she won't eat things that were alive, she'll have a hamburger instead.

We leave the open meadow where grasshoppers, their wings barely dried by the sun, have begun sailing through the grasses. We head up the mountainside where scraggly pines creak in the wind and chunks of shale and limestone litter the zigzagged trails.

"Libby," I say, "Don't go so fast. You'll use up your energy."

"You're supposed to use energy," she replies, not slowing her pace even when she stumbles over a rock. Anna struggles to keep up, and soon they are panting. Still they sing a made-up song, some private collaboration they've been working on all weekend. I only ever hear scraps of words, and I sometimes believe they are singing the lyrics out of order so I won't understand. But they're only seven and five.

I hear *the sun popped, la la la,* and what sounds like *jumbleberries.* Then I'm listening to the wind tease the trees, sticks snapping beneath my soles, hearing in my head James tickling his squealing girls before bed, after he accused me of helping them cheat at cards. "They've got to learn how to lose, Natalie. It's a tough lesson, but a necessary one."

"You would know," I snapped. "You've learned your loser lessons well."

Our short, tense argument on the red front porch that still smells of new paint, words hissed in low, venomous tones so the girls wouldn't know. The long, silent night until the screen door creaked just past four. Clomp of waders suddenly muffled as he stepped off the porch and into a moonless night. The cards stay in small piles on the table. The hands wait to be played.

"Look," Libby announces. "Deer poop." I remember how she's been here before with her father, and now I wish I could teach them something on this trip, something useful they will always remember. We gather around the pile of brown beads, a dewy sheen still on them.

"It's fresh. If you're very quiet, we may see deer."

Anna's eyes grow round and she clamps her hand to her mouth, trying so hard not to shout her excitement, but Libby asks—loudly—how I know it's fresh. Sometimes I encourage her defiance of silence, her refusal to submit to good-girl behavior. Today I hold my finger to my lips, my eyes narrowed in what must pass for stern. She asks again, more softly, so I tell her to smell it.

"Gross!" She whirls and races up the slope. Anna, already tired, stays with me, and I am oddly touched when she takes my hand.

"Margaret always looked for deer poop. But I don't know why," she says, almost to herself.

"Who?" Their mother's name is Gabrielle, but she's hacked it to Gabi because her new fiancé prefers it and wants the children to call her that too. The fiancé's name is Jimbo, which James despises for how it mocks his own solid, full name. He hates nicknames and resents that Libby won't ever answer to Elizabeth.

"Daddy's girlfriend before you," she says matter-of-factly. "She couldn't cut it." I want to laugh at that phrase in her five-year-old mouth, but something in it makes me angry. I can't even remember what he said about Margaret. Was she the outfitter or the bookseller? I don't think I've heard her name before, and I've known James since before Christmas.

"Can you?" She's staring up at me with those pretty green eyes, and before I can answer, Libby's startled shout distracts us both. She's ten yards ahead and facing a man with a rifle.

"Hey there," he calls, his face friendly but keen. "What are you all doing up here?"

Libby is frozen, in awe of his weapon, but Anna answers with a sigh, "We're looking for deer poop." The man chuckles. His face doesn't. Long lines cut his stubbled cheeks vertically— the face of a boulder with freeze cracks and moss, like he's come from the very mountain itself.

"Better do that somewhere else," he advises. "I'm on the trail of a mountain lion."

Libby is still shocked into an unusual, gaping quiet, but Anna gasps a silly little-girl gasp that I wish I'd inspired with some incredible fact. I can't help it; I want her to adore me.

"What do you mean you're on the trail of it?" The girls have nodded their heads together to whisper excitedly, and the tracker leans in like we're our own conspiracy. I smell bitter coffee on his breath.

"Attacked an old man by the river yesterday morning. I'm surprised you didn't hear the scream."

"I don't remember any screams. But we didn't arrive until after noon."

"You'd remember if you heard," the tracker says. "They scream like a murdered lady, those cats."

"The cats scream?" By now the girls are trying to listen to our conversation, and I instinctively lower my voice.

"You never heard one then, have you? Chills your blood. You'd best get those kids back to their cabin. Mountain lions are attracted to little ones."

The girls chase each other with dead pine branches, their squeals pitched unnervingly high.

I look down at the girls and the golden hair that captures light even in this dense pocket of trees. Their hair glistens like spinners in the river. Bait. I scan the area for lions as if one would be waiting in plain sight, fork and knife in paw.

"What happened to the old man?" I ask, unable to resist the gruesome pictures in my head, the mangled limbs floating downstream.

"Stitches on his neck and back," says the tracker. "Might have been killed if his wife hadn't shot at it." He brandishes his rifle, and then, as if remembering his purpose, pretends to tip the hat he isn't wearing, and tells the girls to be good and listen to their mama. Then he's off, striding purposely up the side of the mountain at a right angle to our own path. A vigilante, his only authority the weapon in his hand.

Listen to your mama, girls. Listen to her tell why each and every one of your father's girlfriends can't make the cut. Then I'm wondering if maybe James is the one who tells them this, if I'm being tested right now. For a single, wildly paranoid moment I suspect the lion tracker has been hired, the grizzled extra in a Ted Turner made-for-television movie. Not even that good of an actor.

I come to my senses. "Come on, girls, we're going back. Now." I herd them in front of me and give each a short, firm push forward.

"But we didn't see the murdered lady," Libby complains, still watching the tracker retreat.

"Who got murdered?" Anna face puckers with worry.

"No one," I say firmly. "But we need to go. And be quiet. No. Make noise." I try to remember whether mountain lions are scared off by noise. "Yes, be noisy." Libby whoops and jumps hard on a stick, obliterating the sounds of birdsong and any huge, padded feet behind us. I whirl to nothing but trees and rocks and a forest floor smothered in brown pine needles. "Quieter than that," I add.

We've not gone far on our return path when Anna, short of breath, calls over her shoulder to me. "Natalie...do lions...do they...eat...people?"

I stop walking and peek around me. I decide she may as well know the truth. Not to shield, not to baby.

The sun strums the golden meadow... the girls chase each other.

"Yes, sweetheart, they do. Especially children." She sucks in her breath, and Libby turns to see if I'm serious, her small face pale as a mushroom. Seized by guilt, I add, "But if we just keep moving, we won't have any problems."

We've only walked another hurried ten yards when Libby stops and says, "What about our daddy?"

Now it is his mangled body I imagine floating down the river, the arm he didn't put around my shoulders last night caught in a low-floating branch, waving an aborted goodbye.

Anna starts to whimper, alarmed by something in my face, and I don't even attempt to tell them stories about how Daddy could kill a mountain lion with his bare hands. Sometimes he fishes with headphones on, playing George Winston because he claims that music charms the fish right through the line. He would never hear the scream. But then I don't know if mountain lions scream when they attack or before or just when they need attention.

"Come on," I urge the kids, "Run." Later, I will read that this is the worst thing to do when trying to avoid the notice of a mountain lion. But I needed out of the forest, off the mountain, into the clearing where our small rental cabin warmed in the morning sunlight.

We shuttle down the trail, nearly to the clearing when Anna, tired Anna, trips, rolls, and smashes into the trunk of a tree. She wails in pain, and I think that if the lion hasn't noticed us before, well, here we are, advertisements for fast food.

"Shhh, hush now." I squat beside her and see blood spreading rapidly from a cut in her scalp, staining and matting her pretty hair, more blood on both knees, dirt everywhere. Libby is already ahead, in the clearing, and when she turns, I see in the sunlight that her face is glistening with tears too. Shiny silver spinners.

"Libby," I call. "Come help me?"

She doesn't even shake her head to tell me no. She runs on, disappears around the corner of the cabin.

"Shhh. Shhh. It's okay," I whisper. I pick Anna up and settle her bloody, dirty body against me. I carry her into the clearing where the sun claims us again. Only her golden hair is pink at the ends where blood and tears have mingled. And she's heavy.

James speeds around the corner like he's being chased. His eyes are intense and fixed on us, and I pretend he's running to me, that he'll gather us both in his arms and we'll cling there. But he takes Anna from me, as I know he will, and she falls quiet when his tender fingers probe the wound which, it turns out, is only superficial but will leave a scar like a tiny mouth under her hair.

Libby comes after with the white first aid-kit from the cabin. She carefully hands James the rubbing alcohol, the bandages, the ointments, everything he needs at just the right moment.

"You told them a mountain lion was chasing them?"

"No," I insist. "I only said they were dangerous. Because Anna asked."

James doesn't say anything, just swabs alcohol over the raspberry scrapes on his child's legs.

"We thought you got ate up," his little nurse whispers, and her sister nods solemnly.

"Oh honey, no," he says, kissing them one at a time on their pudgy cheeks. "Your daddy would have chopped up that mean old lion and used him for bait. Then I'd catch the biggest catfish ever." Anna giggles, and Libby tries not to smile. She doesn't want to be comforted just yet.

"There aren't any catfish in this river," I gently remind him. "They like muddy water."

"Fine, spoilsport, we'll have to settle for those pan-sized rainbow trout I brought back."

He seems happy, and the fried fish makes a delicious meal. Anna forgets that she wanted hamburger, and soon, once she starts constructing a pine-branch castle for grasshoppers, she forgets her injuries too. The only clue that the morning started in chaos is that Libby won't leave her father's side, and she carries her walking stick with her, sometimes holding it like a rifle.

Finally, after the girls are in bed, worn out from swimming and playing, we're sipping from beer cans on that blood-red porch. The sky shades toward dark, and James asks why I tried to scare them.

"I didn't try to scare them. That was never my intent." I wanted to teach them something they'd never forget. This is what I don't say.

"Libby's all nervous now. She thinks there are lions out there waiting to gobble us up. She used to have such terrible nightmares."

"There *are* lions out there." I swig my beer for something to do, bitter taste I'd rather pour out. An owl calls through the trees and nothing answers.

"That's not the point," he says, staring off into the trees, a black hairy mass to our left that looks so threatening now, tangled like the forests in fairy tales.

"Was Margaret the bookseller or the outfitter?"

"Margaret?"

I can't believe he doesn't remember her when Anna so clearly does.

"An old girlfriend of yours?" I prompt. "She always looked for deer droppings?"

James laughs, if that's the word for such a stingy sound. "You mean Sylvia. She bought a book on animal tracks and scat before we brought her out here. She carried it with her on all our hikes, and her fingers smelled like shit because she'd break open droppings to see what the animal had been eating. That's when I volunteered to prepare all the meals."

"So who was Margaret?"

"The bookseller. She probably sold Sylvia the shit book." That laugh again.

The girls chase each other with dead pine branches.

"Which one came first?"

"Why does it matter?"

I don't have a good answer, so I finish my beer, crumple the can, and ask, "Why do all your exes have three-syllable names?"

Even in the purple dusk I can see he's looking at me like I'm crazy, so I run aloud through the list I know: Gabrielle, Margaret, Sylvia, Bethany, Natalie, not necessarily in that order.

"I don't know," he scoffs. "Name length isn't one of my criteria."

What is your criteria anyway? Another question that stays buried.

Very softly, I say, "You could call me Nat sometimes. I like that."

The laugh again. Third time not a charm. "What? So you could marry a *Jimbo* too? I don't like Nat. It sounds as frivolous as *Gabi*."

"Shhhhhhh." I press my finger to his mouth, and his eyes, hollows in the shadows of the coming night, open wide like he's trying to see me in the dark.

"Can't you hear it?" I ask. *Last, unclawed moment.*

He shakes his head no. I keep my finger to his mouth like a stitch.

"Screams," I say. "I'm sure I hear screams."

ALL THE BIRDS VANISH

They've lied to her. All the self-help books, her friends, even her mother. They all claimed she'd emerge from her divorce a stronger woman—the clichéd butterfly bursting from her cocoon. Savannah, a co-worker with a master's in guidance counseling, cheered her on: "No one's saying it's easy, but you'll become your true self. Just wait and wait beautifully!"

Helen is still waiting, because she doesn't want this self to be her. She's let her hair grow out more, she's taken to vegetarian cuisine in Montana beef country, and she's found some solace in gardening. She doesn't mind any of these things about herself. Her son says she's prettier with long hair and she feels healthier without meat, especially after all those *E. coli* scares. These trappings may be part of a self she couldn't share with her husband, but they've come at the price of secret fears she never knew she had and a pervasive sense of weakness she doesn't confess aloud until her son is asleep. Then, in the bathtub, scrubbing her skin with oatmeal soap and mumbling a litany of her failures, she cries and feels better, if only for a while. Always she looks in on Sam after, to assure herself that he's safely sleeping, oblivious. This ritual makes her feel like a proper parent.

Helen has decided, in the absence of a family stability she'd once taken for granted, that Sam is her personal mission. He is the reason she works with the special education kids. Money and benefits, a worldly exchange that can put him through college and buy him a head start, all the opportunities her students will never have. She would like to think she works with these students out of compassion. She doesn't mind when others assume as much. But in truth they wear her out and sometimes she secretly loathes the ones who wrap their thin arms around her in needy hugs, something that Corey Dunham does up to ten times a day. Then, recognizing her own shameful disgust, she turns it on herself, waits for the moment she can slide into the too-hot water and soak her sins away. Helen spoils her own son in the meantime. She doesn't question this thin umbilicus between her students and son, just acts on it. When she is a bad mother, she is an indulgent teacher, and vice versa.

Now, convinced her son is slipping away from her, she's taken to hugging the kids at school back, bringing Life Savers to slip in their pockets. Corey likes the peppermint kind and he will sit quietly and stop fighting with the other kids when she flashes him the shiny blue roll. And he's stopped clinging to her this week. He accepts her hugs and goes on to do his work. All he needed, she thinks guiltily, is genuine affection. But her training reminds her that it's much more complicated than that. Next week he will bite Brandy Kamrath again, he will refuse to follow directions, and he will cry even when she hugs him back. She knows all this even as she pretends some measure of control.

She doesn't know what Sam will do next week either. He's been acting up, sulking in ways that her good-natured son doesn't. She's tried to attribute it to puberty, but this seems another weak attempt to explain one's life away, and Helen has come to despise simple solutions as much as she longs for them.

Nick is partly to blame. Helen can't deny this. What she can't figure out as she sips her nightly chamomile tea, soothing her insides after her bath, is why he's doing this now.

She's been divorced for some time, and it was years before that, at least three, when she made that mistake. Her only indiscretion in a long marriage, one for which she could easily forgive herself if she could only explain it. She's never been attracted to her gun-toting neighbor. She's never liked the way he leers and says cruel things when he's uncomfortable. And she'd been good friends with his wife back when they were both raising baby boys while their husbands worked. All of it now, still, such a mystery. She doesn't remember the woman she was before the divorce, not really, and she still doesn't recognize the one she is now. *Just wait and enjoy the unfolding*, Savannah tells her. *Wait.*

Sam still tells her he loves her at night, right after she flicks off his light. Not everything can be lost if he's still sensitive enough to say the words, she assures herself, something she also believed about Alan as he packed his bags to leave their family. Savannah says, "He's a kid, Helen. You put way too much stock in what he says and does. You need an adult man around."

Savannah Says. A children's game or advice column. But her co-worker and best friend is almost always right. Helen feels the tidal tug of loneliness on her heart at night. But she knows that man Savannah says she needs never was and never will be Nick, and she doesn't like how close he's getting to her son.

Helen knows that Nick Burns encourages her son to try the weight of guns in his small hand, to draw a bead on a bird or a knot in a tree. She trusts that the guns are never loaded. Nick isn't stupid with weapons. She also knows how Sam has disobeyed her direct order against Hunter's Safety class. Helen is a perceptive woman and what she misses intuitively she picks up by snooping, a tactic she's always been able to justify because she enjoys it so much. And Sam has no practice with dishonesty. He's no good at it.

The time hasn't come to call him on his lies yet, Helen thinks as she rinses out her teacup and slowly wipes up the crumbs around the toaster. She's a strategist, some survival skill that developed around the time of her divorce. She is learning to wait.

Sam appears in the kitchen, backpack slung over one shoulder.

"Ready?" she asks, and he stares a second before muttering something that sounds like "duh."

After she's dropped Sam at school, Helen picks up Savannah, who is the district coordinator of special education and has an office in the school where Helen teaches. Savannah has been married twice and now dates an odd assortment of professional men from lawyers to a local hockey star. "Sex is less expensive than marriage and more fun," she quips, fluffing her dark brown hair in mock movie-star style. In reality, she is down-to-earth, kind, and convinced that she always knows what she wants—all attributes that draw Helen to her. They're about the same age, only Savannah doesn't have or want children, which makes her unusual as a native of their small Montana city.

She sips coffee from a red plastic traveler's mug, leaving a purplish stain where her lips kiss the cup, and asks, "How's our Sam today?"

Helen sighs and replies that nothing has changed. "He's gone all the time now that he's made up with Davey. As soon as they get home from school, they disappear to ride bikes or hang out anywhere but my house."

"Why don't you tell him he can't do that? You're the parent."

Helen stops at a traffic light and winces when she hears the brakes cry out for service. She hates when people without children tell people with children how to parent. Helen shrugs. "*You're* the parent," Savannah repeats.

During lunch, Helen stays in the sunny classroom to eat her cheese sandwich. She likes time for quiet reflection during the day. Without it, she feels slightly mad, like she could go off on anyone at anytime. The decorations will need to be changed soon. Traced-hand turkeys, hers the largest, soon to be replaced with two-dimensional ornaments glued with glitter and pasted over with a snapshot of each child. Maybe real pine branches on the bulletin board? A tree for the room? Or is that a fire hazard? Mental note to talk to Dianne, the secretary, about it. And more glue sticks for projects.

She is thinking about the Thanksgiving holiday and what she'll cook if her parents don't come up (is there such a thing as vegetarian turkey?) when Brandy Kamrath comes into the room, doe eyes glossy with tears. Her silence unnerves Helen. She looks like a poster for starving or neglected children except that Brandy is far from starving. Her cheeks are smooth, fat curves, her knees dimpled. A Kewpie doll.

"What is it, hon?" Helen wraps up the crusts of her sandwich and tosses them in the empty trash along with her soda can, startling Brandy, who then starts to make noise, small strangled mews.

She won't say what's bothering her no matter how much Helen coaxes. Brandy just wants to be held, and when Helen's patience thins, the girl sits at the coloring table, sniffing, a green crayon poised idly in her fist. Savannah walks in, her heels clopping a welcome beat.

"Hi, Brandy!" she chirps when she sees the little girl. "Why aren't you outside on lunch recess?"

Brandy shrugs and sniffs, but a smile plays at the corner of her mouth. The kids always love Savannah's attention because she's loud and bright and naturally affectionate. "Go on," she urges. "You've got ten minutes of recess left. Soon the snow will come, and you'll be stuck inside."

This tactic doesn't work. Brandy sinks into herself, and in her eerie, formal way of speaking, says, "I will stay in here."

"Suit yourself," Savannah replies with one last wink before turning to Helen. "You need to call the middle-school principal. She left a message for you in the office."

"Mrs. Banks? Why? Is Sam okay?"

"She didn't say it was urgent, but why don't you go call now? I'll stay with Brandy and see if I can get her to talk to me."

"You just want to know what's up, Snoop," Helen says, standing to leave.

"Of course. I almost majored in journalism. I wanted to be Barbara Walters."

Helen thanks her and walks quickly to the main office, trying not to look as alarmed as she feels. The principal has never called before.

"A gun?" Stunned, Helen repeats the words aloud, and Dianne sneaks a look from behind her computer screen. "Where would he get a gun? Are you sure it was his?"

"We aren't sure of anything right now. The boys aren't talking and I've had no choice but to expel them. Temporarily of course. But you will need to come get Sam. I'm not letting him return to class."

"For how long?"

"Two weeks' suspension. I know the weapon wasn't loaded, but it was still a weapon. And you've seen the news. You know why we take this very seriously. Some school districts would expel him permanently." Mrs. Banks' voice is apologetic, aware that Sam has always been a bright, trouble-free student.

"I understand. I really do. I mean I don't understand *this,* but I know why you have to punish them. Does Davey need a ride?"

"David's mother has already picked him up."

After explaining as best she can to Savannah and her principal, Helen leaves her kids in the care of a teacher's aide. One little boy, William John, starts to cry when she says she's leaving. He is ten years old and does this every morning his father drops him off, and she shocks herself and most of the classroom when she says sharply, "Stop it." He stops, brown eyes wide, mouth agape with spittle threads, and she nearly sprints through the narrow halls, eager to leave the crying and the chaos behind her like an itchy skin that can be permanently shed and abandoned.

Sam is sullen, but his eyes betray fear and a hint of amazement at his predicament. He is slumped in an overstuffed chair outside the principal's office, and with his freckles, mussed hair, and defiant expression, he looks like a Norman Rockwell painting, something titled "An Afternoon at the Principal's Office."

"Sam?" Her voice comes out more gently than expected. "What's going on?"

"Nothing." The single most maddening response a child can give a parent. Ordinarily, Helen wouldn't put up with it. But fear and confusion have melted her backbone away, and she wants to collapse.

"Okay," she replies, her bright voice garish and artificial, a fake flower on a lapel. She can smell the dusty plastic of it, the desperate attempt to hide how shabby and insubstantial she feels. "We can talk about it later."

Mrs. Banks peeks out from her office to summarize the punishment. He can return to classes two weeks from tomorrow, and of course he'll have to make up all the missed work. Helen agrees to pick up assignments for him, while Sam just stares at his scuffed sneakers. He says nothing when his principal tells him to take care.

"Cat got your tongue?" Helen asks when they get in the car.

"I didn't do anything wrong." Every child says this at some point, but Sam sounds like he believes it.

"Then what happened? How did you end up with a handgun in your locker? A *handgun*, Sam. Because I don't understand that part. I really don't." Her voice inflates in sudden anger, and she bangs the steering wheel, light punctuation. Her throat stings, and tears well.

Sam squirms in his seat, adjusts his seatbelt as if to emphasize that they should move out of the gravel parking lot, and shrugs. "Davey brought it. He wanted to put it in my locker and I said fine."

"Fine? You said that was *fine*?"

"Jeez, Mom. I wasn't gonna use it. Davey was just going to show it to some kid that's been picking on him. You know, scare him."

"And the slingshot Mrs. Banks showed me? Was that yours?" Helen watches the morning-session kindergarten kids push out of the side doors and run to waiting parents or buses. All of them, boys and girls, wear bright, festive colors and cartoon characters on their backpacks. Little ornaments livening up the afternoon.

"Sort of. Me and Davey share it. It's for shooting at trees and stuff."

"Trees, huh? Why were these things in *your* locker? You know it got you an extra week's suspension, and if the gun hadn't been there, they probably wouldn't have even thought of the slingshot as a weapon. Really dumb choices here."

"It *is* a weapon. It can kill prairie dogs."

"I don't need to hear that." She has an unusual sensitivity to killing animals, even accidentally. Once, after clipping a stray cat on a busy street, she'd wept most of the night while Alan persisted in asking what was wrong. He refused to accept that a dead cat could account for her misery. He asked if she was hiding something which should have been her first clue to his own deception. "What did Davey's father have to do with this mess?"

"Nick?"

Helen's jaw clenches to hear the familiar first name. "You'll call him Mr. Burns. That's more respectful." Not, she thinks, that the man deserves any respect. She unbuckles her seatbelt and shuffles out of her coat. Too hot in the car with the autumn sunshine baking the interior, too chilly outside with the Great Falls wind.

"*Mr. Burns* doesn't have anything to do with it. Davey swiped the gun. He was going to return it. It's not like anybody got hurt."

"The whole point is that someone could have."

Helen says this aloud to scare herself with the possibilities. She knows that Sam understands the potential danger more than he's letting on. She cranks the engine to life, letting this be the last parental profundity from her mouth for a while.

They ride in silence. Helen immediately turns off the radio when Sam flips it on, and he doesn't try again.

Driving, she thinks about what could have happened. A dangerous game, this speculation. She used to think about what could have happened if she and Alan hadn't divorced. All that ever did was make her believe alternately that either she was a bitch or he was a bastard. Somebody had to have ruined it. But to think this way only led to depressive bouts then a fresh cycle of old blame. She let it go finally, somehow, and now she's only jealous when she thinks of his new wife and new baby on the way. I'm miles away from that, she thinks. Miles. *Just wait.* Savannah says. *Wait.* For what?

What could have happened is that the gun could have been loaded, someone could have been shot either accidentally or on purpose, and that someone could have been Sam. Helen indulges in the imagined scene of a small casket at a small funeral where Alan, with a spray of lilies at his back, tells her he's sorry for everything. It's a childish fantasy, this vengeance through death and an eternity of blame, and so Helen abandons the thought, struggles to abandon it, because it's so seductive, and asks Sam where he wants to eat.

"You're taking me out for lunch?"

"Aren't you hungry?"

"Yeah, but I just got busted for having a gun in my locker. Most parents would make me eat liver."

"I don't cook meat, as you well know, and I don't think they have a fast-food liver joint yet, so that's lucky for you. So where?"

"McDonald's."

Helen, thinking of cows lined up dumbly for a skull-bashing, sighs. A tasteless garden salad and a diet Coke. Her emergency menu for such occasions. She turns onto Tenth Avenue South, heading for the corporate golden arches, wondering why she gives in so easily.

"I don't know what to do with you." It's 7:30 a.m., and Helen hasn't thought about what it means that Sam can't go to school until just this minute. She won't leave him alone, not all day. It would be like making his punishment into some sort of playday. "What is Jill doing with Davey?"

"I don't know. I'm not allowed to talk to him, remember?"

"Not for awhile, no. Hmm. Is Mrs. Gibson still staying at home during the day?"

"How should I know? I don't like her kids anyway."

"Sam."

"Bess tried to kiss me last time I walked past their yard."

"How gruesome," Helen says. "Even so, I can't take you with me."

"Why not? I can read or something. The retarded kids don't bother me."

"They're not *retarded*." Helen pours the black dregs of the coffee pot into a thermos and pulls the plug from the outlet. "They mostly have emotional problems."

"So? Everybody has those."

Sometimes Helen is surprised at how grown-up her son seems at age twelve. So smart. She hopes he inherited it from her, but then Alan, despite his many flaws, is no idiot. "Okay," she says. "You'll come to school with me."

Savannah looks surprised to see her son in the backseat, disappointed at the lost opportunity to discuss his predicament with Helen. "Hi, Sam," she says as though he's just another employee in the carpool. At the door to Helen's classroom, Savannah whispers, "You're really taking him to class?"

"Why not?"

Savannah purses her lips then throws her hands up. "Why not?"

The kids are agitated about someone new invading their space. They stare at Sam, who quietly reads a science-fiction comic, pretending not to notice that he is the center of their attention. When Helen tries to engage them in addition exercises, the kids make silly mistakes and continue to glance at Sam as though he has answers to bestow upon those most faithful in their attentions.

Five minutes before the first recess, she gives up and lets them go early, hoping they'll get the best equipment and keep it when the other kids, made bold by their status as "normal" students, try to intimidate them. The kids go reluctantly, looking to Sam as if he's supposed to accompany them. By now, Helen has explained that he is her son, and for some reason this fascinates them all the more. All except Corey, the hugger, who reacts with a pout and some angry mumbling to himself.

"Can I go out too?" Sam asks, smiling at two girls who lag behind. They giggle and run out to the hall.

"Not yet. I want to talk to you."

"Oh boy." Sam lays his head on the table where he's sitting, follows it with a dramatic sigh that makes her smile.

"How's the comic book?"

"Fine."

"Oh, fine yourself. Go out. You've earned a recess. We'll talk later."

"Thanks, Mom." Sam pats her on the arm and races out the door.

She doesn't know what she wanted to talk to him about anyway. Recess is only ten minutes long, and she still hasn't decided how to approach the gun in the locker. But she also feels that the longer she waits, the more she's sending the message that the incident isn't important. When to wait, when to tackle? Mostly Helen just wants him to know that she wants to talk. That seems most important now.

They get a chance to talk later that evening, but not about what she'd planned. Sam initiates. "Mom, something's kind of bugging me." She's seen him all afternoon and early evening, disturbed wrinkles on his brow and around his mouth, and she's chalked it up to either guilt or annoyance about sitting in on her class.

"Talk to me," she says, setting aside her magazine.

"I don't like how that boy in your class bothers that girl."

"What boy and what girl? I'm not following you." She hoped to hear him truly confess his part in the gun incident so they could move past that, past Nick Burns, past whatever has disrupted her formerly strong bond with her son. Now he's avoiding the topic all over again.

"Corey and Brandy. You know." He squirms, more uncomfortable, looking like he wished he'd never brought it up.

"No, I don't know. What's Corey doing? Calling her names again?"

"No."

"Biting her arm? Her ear? Drawing blood?"

"No."

"Then what, Sam? You brought this up." Her frustration mounts. This isn't the conversation she wanted, and the article on the re-introduction of the Mexican gray wolf is drawing her back. Some terrorist shooting them dead. A pup died trying to suckle its cold mother. She wants to return to those four pages that can contain and direct and absorb all her free-floating rage and fear.

"He pushes a stick at her face and her private parts." Sam blushes and picks at a cuticle until it bleeds, but he tumbles forward with all he wants to say. "I saw on recess. He makes her go around the building and pokes at her, and she just stands there and cries until he goes away."

Helen's first thought is how that kid hugged her all those times, never meaning anything by it. Empty gestures hiding a mean heart. Then she thinks of Brandy, those fat tears, Helen pushing her to go outside. Or was that Savannah doing the pushing? She doesn't remember, but feels the guilt regardless, a nauseous flood of it.

"Oh God," Helen says. "I thought she was just being a baby. She cries when the dispenser is out of paper towels. They all cry. Over crayons, over math problems, over everything." She feels like crying herself.

Sam shrugs, keeps his eyes down like he's embarrassed, and she thinks to pat his leg and thank him for telling her. Then she adds, "Don't tell anyone else, okay?" He nods, relieved by the imposed silence on a topic he doesn't like.

That night in the hot bath Helen tries to think how to handle this new situation. A chubby girl with outstretched arms like French bread loaves, bright against the dark brick of the school. A stick, muddy and broken, probing and staining her skin. Wet eyes turned up to the cold, cloudless sky. Angry parents, at least two sets, accusing her of negligence. Of doing nothing. She scrubs furiously at a callous on her heel, finally accepts that it's not sloughing off, and soaks so long that her hands pucker. She imagines herself an old, old woman and gets out of the tub in slow motion, mindful of slipping. She acts this way the rest of the evening, as though careful attention is an art to be practiced, something she hopes will manifest itself in her daily life and make her wise.

Alan calls the next evening. Just as she's done nothing about the gun in the locker, Helen hasn't approached the Brandy situation except to spend recess outside with the kids. Accumulating loose threads.

"I'm glad you answered the phone, Helen." She hates how he behaves when his new wife is in the same room. He doesn't have to say she's there. Helen knows. "I wanted to ask if you'd thought about dates for Christmas yet. We need to get the plane ticket soon."

Of course she hasn't thought about it. She's been trying to forget that she's losing her son at Christmas. She hasn't even figured out Thanksgiving plans with her parents yet.

"Can you give me a few more days on that? I've been busy."

"Well, just a few. I really need to get that set. It's late to be buying tickets, and with the baby coming and all, our finances are stretched."

Yes, yes, she knows about stretches. "I'll figure it out soon, promise."

"Okay. So how have you been?"

Gee, Alan, thanks for asking. "Fine. Busy, like I said."

"I guess we're all busy. That's life, huh?"

"Life, right. I'd forgotten what one was." She meant to keep the sarcasm out of her voice this time. Another failure to add to the list. "I'll get Sam."

She listens to them talk while she idles over a crossword puzzle. Keeps thinking: *I should tell Alan about the gun in the locker.* Keeps thinking: *This is between my son and me. Alan left.* And when she realizes that Sam has hung up without saying a word of his trouble, she takes it as a sign that he feels the same way.

"How's your dad?"

"Fine," Sam says. "Just fine."

Still Sam goes to school with her to read and catch up on homework. Still Helen says nothing about the gun incident, almost as if her son is on vacation rather than suspended, almost as if when the two weeks is over, so is her need to worry. But once the first week is up and Davey Burns is back in school, she feels the prickle of injustice, and finally she calls the Burns family to get the story.

A Friday night. Sam downstairs watching music videos, something Helen allows as a weekend treat. Normally she can't stand the vulgar images and blaring noise, but she also understands that it's a part of growing up these days. She can only hope he'll decide for himself that these videos are stupid and repetitive.

She has to look up the number in the phone book. She knew it by heart back when she and Jill Burns were friends. The less they talked, the further into her mind's recesses went the numbers, from a mixed-up 9 and 6 to the guessed-at prefix until it vanished altogether. *That's* life, Alan. Mix-ups, guessing, vanishing.

Helen dials, hoping that either Jill or Davey will answer.

"Helen? Well, it's been a long time." His voice is neutral, cautious, giving nothing away.

"I know. I just wanted to talk to you and Jill about the boys' suspension."

"What about it?"

"I wondered where they got the gun." She says it quickly, trying not to sound accusatory.

Nick says, "How should I know? Kids can get guns anywhere these days."

"You haven't asked Davey about it?"

"Of course I did. He says Sam brought it."

"That's ridiculous," Helen snaps, knowing in her heart that the weapon came from the Burns' home.

"Look, I believe what my kid tells me. It's not my problem if your son lies to you."

"Go to hell! Everyone in this neighborhood knows who the gun nut is."

"Calm down," he says. "You sound like you're having some problems raising Sam alone." Then, the final jab. "If you ever need any help, Helen, you know Jill and I would be glad to assist. Just give us a call."

By now she is shaking with fury. She remembers the night she walked over to his house, wanting little Sam back from his first planned sleepover at Davey's. She'd found a note from Alan's lover that same evening. They'd fought, Alan had gone to a motel for the night, and then she needed, like a physical hunger, someone in her bed breathing a soft loving sound her way. She'd climbed the back fence to the alley and slipped through the Burns' gate, around the house and to their front door. She'd meant to get Sam, bring him home under some false pretense, and tuck him into her bed where she could smell his little-boy sweetness.

Nick had answered the door. The boys were in the fort outside because it was a warm night, and Jill, who Helen most wanted to talk to, had gone to bed early with a migraine. Nick had listened, not seeming the slightest bit uncomfortable when the tears poured forth. One solid hug became a squeeze became a face nuzzled in a neck, and the rest of it happened behind the closed door of the den on a vinyl couch with glassy-eyed buck heads the only witnesses.

She remembers imagining her husband alone in a motel room. And the flame of self-satisfaction stretching in her belly. And how she'd started to hate Nick Burns, who called her once after to see if she wanted to come over for a beer. "Go to hell," she'd said then. "I'm not like that." Then she'd slunk around, avoiding Jill and trying to keep Alan away from the Burnses because they were going to "work on the marriage."

She has nothing to lose now and tells Nick, "It makes me sick to think that you're just a few feet from my property. You're the last person I'd call for anything."

"Well, like someone once said, *Darlin'*, good fences make good neighbors."

"Frost."

"You can say that again."

"Frost," she whispers after he hangs up and the shrill pitch of the dial tone makes her grit her teeth. "Frost."

She walks over to the sink to do the dishes, one of those household tasks that Helen finds relaxing and mind-numbing enough that she can think, or "process" in Savannah-speak. She hears a creak on the stair and turns.

"Sam?"

Suddenly he's there rooting through cabinets as though he hasn't been eavesdropping. He says all too unconvincingly, "Oh hi, Mom. Just wanted some cookies. Who was on the phone?"

"Savannah."

She slowly wipes the fingerprints from a drinking glass with her sponge. She can hear Sam pause and exhale slowly. She feels his stare. Helen allows herself a small smile because she's beat him. He can't call her on her lie without revealing his own deceit.

She rinses the glass, sets it gingerly in the drying rack. She turns to his stony face.

"Only two cookies," she announces. "Too much sugar will make you sick."

By the end of the weekend, Helen wishes she'd leveled with him about calling the Burnses. He's sullen, more difficult than usual, and she can't confront him without rupturing their facade of trust. So they eat their Sunday casserole in a thick shroud of silence, punctured by occasional niceties. *Please pass the pepper. Are there any napkins?* Helen starts to tell Sam a funny story about a friend who asked for a napkin at a restaurant in London. But she pauses at the punch line, realizing that mention of sanitary napkins will only embarrass and anger her adolescent son. It's not the first time she's wished for a daughter, someone to share the little inconveniences of her gender.

At recess the next day Sam teaches the children an optical illusion. He makes it look like he's pulling his own thumb off. He completes the trick with a popping sound and a grimace that makes Helen, still mad at them both, laugh too. Once the children realize it's only a trick, they spend the rest of the day pulling off their own thumbs. And the illusion is new to them every time, freshly funny enough to make the same kids squeal, distracting them from learning. Corey seems to like it better than anyone.

"Look, look," he yells at her for the third time that afternoon. "My thumb popped off!"

She gives him a stern look, one eyebrow raised to say *I'm sick of this already.* What she really wants to say is *I wish it would pop off. If I had a daughter, I'd never let you near her, you someday sex offender.* In the week since she learned of his abuse of Brandy, she's concluded that he's a lost cause, that nothing she does will make any difference. She's separated the children into two play groups for recess: boys and girls. They aren't allowed to cross over, and so far everyone's obeyed. She likes seeing the careful clusters of girls whirling the tetherball, the tangled knots of boys running on the field, the wide borders of blacktop between. In her mind Helen has solved the problem for as long as these students are in her class. And that, she decides, is the extent of her responsibility.

Sam is another matter altogether. Her responsibility for life. She can't bring herself to think he's a someday gun man.

Aware of the hypocrisy, Helen can only tell herself that blood calls for a whole different criteria by which to judge. Then she turns the hot-water knob a little higher when she takes a bath, just to see how much blush her skin can stand.

When the weekend arrives, Helen tells Sam that they are taking a picnic lunch to the Fort Benton Wildlife Preserve to go bird-watching before winter sets in and all the birds vanish. Though of course they don't all vanish, just the ones she keeps meaning to watch. Geese have begun migrating, and she hopes to see wide, strong, elastic bands of them heading for warmer climates.

"Bring your binoculars," she calls, slapping a spoonful of raspberry preserves onto a thin spread of peanut-buttered bread.

Silence.

"Sam, did you hear me?"

Helen turns and there he is, looking at her with a pained expression on his face.

"Oh, Sam." She can see that he's lost the binoculars, their absence scribed into his face. "You didn't have them very long."

"I'm sorry." He whispers it, waits, his face suspended in sorrow.

"Just get ready. Go. Maybe I'll buy you another pair for Christmas."

"I won't even be here then."

For a moment, right before she remembers his trip to his father's, the words sound ominous. Helen presses the butter knife into the bread, tearing a tiny hole that oozes with raspberry jelly and stains the soft bread around.

At Fort Benton, they button their coats against a chill wind, and position themselves on the old car hood. "That's what I like about these old cars," Helen says. "They're sturdy. The newer plastic cars would just dent under our butts."

Sam giggles, still delighted whenever his mother says a word that's not supposed to be funny to adults. Butts. Usually she chides his immaturity, trying to force it out of him for good, but now she giggles too. He is her little boy again. No Nick, no Davey, no guns or slingshots or children doing things that shouldn't even happen to adults. Helen, Sam, and the birds. A pair of wood ducks on the drive by the lake, some sort of cormorant or egret (she can't tell without the binoculars), and a spiraling ribbon of Canada geese that tickle the winter-bound sky until it expels another cold laugh through their hair.

"It's cold," Sam complains. "And there could be hunters out here."

"Not on a wildlife refuge," Helen scoffs, annoyed that he isn't enjoying this the way she wants him to. She feels alive in the cold wind, likes the rub of it against her cheeks. "Find us some more geese, Sam. They're good luck."

"Why?"

Helen shrugs because she's made it up, something that sounded magical. "Because they mate for life is why. So every time a hunter bangs one down, he's killing love. That's bad luck for certain. Remember that. Look and tell me when you see them coming." Sam tucks his head into his shoulders to ward off the wind's chill and scoots to his edge of the car, his feet swinging rhythmically against the front tire, his eyes fixed upwards.

Perched on the hood of the old car, Helen tilts her head into the wind. Her hair sweeps across her face, strands of it sticking painfully to her eyes, and she wonders if this is how her life will always be, her son just out of reach, searching the pale skies for luck, herself blindly listening for the gunshot.

GRAY DOGS

Another dating attempt, city park, where a goose—years ago—chased her toddler son, both of them waddling furiously as she laughed. She waits on a swing, carefully, since she's prone to motion sickness. She has to pee. But not badly.

His station wagon pulls into the gravel lot, this psychology professor she met at a bar. Crunch of rock and tire. She stands to wave and a child darts for her swing.

"Hello there," he calls, shutting the driver's door then opening the back. She imagines a tartan blanket, a plastic sack full of ripe apples, a well-chilled bottle of wine to celebrate the turning leaves.

Instead, he gently brings forward into the afternoon sun a stiff, wire leash attached to nothing. An empty collar.

"It's okay, girl," he says in a tender, bedroom voice. "It's just a park. You be a good girl for daddy." He flicks his wrist, and the leash bobbles and surges toward her as if a lively puppy dances there.

"She likes you," he says. "She's usually quite shy. Meet my Trixie Jean."

She remembers how he snapped the peanuts in the bar and dug out the meat without taking his eyes from hers, how he flicked the shells to the floor so purposefully. How she'd liked that. She looks down, through the empty collar, at the taupe dirt where a beetle pauses.

"Hi, Trixie Jean." The beetle scrambles under a stick, and the collar—baby blue, studded with rhinestones that spray rainbows at her feet—seems to wink at her. He waits, as if she's supposed to reach down and scratch behind the ears, pat the invisible rump, gurgle *whatagoodgirl-yes-whatagoodgirl.* She says, "Should we all take a walk on the river trail?" She keeps her eyes on him, the smile she'd found so instantly attractive; she watches the tiny gap between his bottom teeth expand when he says yes.

On the trail, they barely speak. The wind weaves the sun through the trees, and it's as if a thousand black-and-gold butterflies rise and land in the leaves every second. She wants to tell him this, but he is watching the dog collar wiggle through a hole in a tree. Chuckling.

"What made you decide to get a dog?" she asks. Trying.

"The same reasons anyone gets a dog."

"Which are?"

His wrist falls slack, the collar dips to earth. He says, briskly, "I like the companionship." A chipmunk springs past them, but the collar shows no interest.

"Why Trixie Jean?" She persists, waiting for revelation.

He shrugs. "I almost called her Shadow. She follows me everywhere, and her coat's a lovely, deep gray. Don't you think?" He holds the leash out so it trembles. The collar keeps winking: play along, play along, this is only a game.

"When I was depressed once," she says, "I mean real depression, I called it the black dog. I didn't invent it, someone famous did. But my son drowned in a boating accident, and that was how I felt—like a big, black dog was watching me. Like it would never stop stalking and never attack."

She takes a slow breath, and the collar suddenly jumps and strays over to a bush. He says, "The right drugs can make all the difference." Then, "Bad girl!" For a moment it seems he means her, but he is speaking to the collar as it strains to follow something into the undergrowth. How, she wonders, is he sure the dog hasn't already slipped away? The cords of his wrist flex and twist. The wire leash is so stiff that he could never hold his invisible dog in his arms, not with the collar on, never close the way you must hold what you love.

"It was a long time ago," she says. "I really have to pee now."

She hopes they will head back, but he hands her a crumpled tissue from his pocket. "We won't watch."

The professor and his collar wander toward the river. She wants to cry, "Watch! You must always watch," but they've vanished. She squats in the dirt alone, and relieves the pressure. She remembers how in third grade they'd traced and cut out life-size human bodies, how she'd been teased for pinning the paper bladder between the lungs. But it makes sense to her now. The fill and leak. Fill and leak.

The wind kicks up, and as she buttons her pants, she stares up where the sky plays hide-and-seek between leaves, where the sun butterflies dance in the treetops until the wind collapses. Somewhere by the river a child shouts.

THE STROKE OF
MIDNIGHT

She didn't start hating me until she was ten. We were
storybook players before—Goldilocks and her bears
finding their "just right," Little Red Riding Hood feasting from
a picnic basket the wolf never drooled over. Sometimes I
dressed up when I read, blood-red lips for Snow White, black-
penciled brows for her favorite, Cinderella.

*And the wicked stepmother stared at her, heart black with
envy, and said, "No, Cinderella. You will never go to the ball."*

"Never!" I cried, fingers swooping to tickle under the soft
fleece of Bettina's nightgown. "Listen to your wicked
stepmother!"

She protested through giggles. "I'm going and you can't
stop me." When I dimmed her lamp and her daddy kissed
her, she sang, "Good night, Prince Daddy, good night, Wicked
Stepmother. I love you!"

Jonah said I shouldn't encourage that name, that it would
inscribe me to her in negative terms. He talked that way
sometimes. Academic and stern. What he meant was
stereotypes and trouble down the road.

But trouble had stopped somewhere else then, light years
away. We painted her room blue with tiny yellow stars, and

when I dimmed the lamp, it seemed the night disappeared. Bettina asked me to make the stars stay. I bought glow-in-the-dark paint and carefully traced every star with my brush.

The stars stayed aglow, their magic dispelling long after she fell to sleep.

I met Jonah at a costume party. Captain Hook with a cascade of black curls and a jaunty hat. That hook, though plastic and dull, snagged my tail and plucked it off. I was a Playboy bunny, and only later did I discover that Jonah had once teased our party hostess that he would only settle down when he found a Playboy bunny with brains. It was a set-up, and the hostess was delighted that he caught me first.

"Fate," she threatened when she called the next day. A word that gives me shivers.

At the party I brought Jonah martinis on a tin platter I scrounged from the kitchen. I wiggled my nose and pretended to be scared when he brandished his hook. I begged for my tail, but he tied it to his belt loop like a scalp or a pelt. He teased in his loud captain's voice, "Bunny, you're going to have to work for it."

And everyone saw then and there how we would fall in love.

I drank the martinis because he preferred beer—"ale, lassy, ale"—and my heart surged with hope. Thirty-three and towing a line of heartbreaks, each worse than the one before, I was nearly resigned to getting a dog, faithful and always there.

After Tate, the rehab counselor, I'd actually walked through the pet store, watching two beagle pups chew each other's ears. He'd left me after three years for one of his former clients, a heroin addict I'd heard so much about that I thought of her as family, some crazy distant cousin. It never dawned on me until much later that he'd broken confidentiality only with that client, some guilty impulse toward confession. Then one day he packed his self-help books, saying, "She needs me. You've never been an addict, Jamie. Your life is so…" He struggled for the word. "So *clean*."

I looked around the gutted apartment, our possessions sorted into piles that kept collapsing. I said, "Congratulations on another successful recovery."

The gin rocketed to my head until I couldn't stop laughing. Jonah carried me to his motorcycle, crushed my bunny ears into his helmet, and drove me to my door.

"You're a lucky bunny," he said. "I don't let just anyone on my bike."

"No?" I toyed with the long fingers he'd hidden all night under that hook.

"I don't get to ride much. When I do, it's a treat. Time to think, wind through my hair." He flipped the ends of his pirate's wig.

"I like your hair." I nuzzled my face in his villainous curls.

"I like your tail." He squeezed the puff still tied to his belt.

Two weeks later, when I was already enchanted, he told me about his daughter. I said, "I love little girls."

Turns out I did love Bettina. It was easy in the beginning when painted stars and a willingness to make believe was all I needed. But trouble always arrives. By then Jonah and I had been married almost three years and only once in all that time had the Real Mother made contact. Christmas morning and the woman on the other end of the phone was slurring and sobbing so Bettina didn't even know what she was saying. Jonah's face tensed like I'd never seen, like he wanted to snatch the phone away and slam it down in permanent disconnection.

After hanging up, Bettina simply said, "That was my mom. She misses me." Then she went back to the chemistry set she'd just opened. Jonah worked at the hospital, analyzing blood and urine under a microscope, a job he loved, and his gift card explained that one day Bettina too could save lives. But she only wanted to dust for Santa's fingerprints, suspicious already that he didn't exist.

Jonah was afraid she'd come back. The Real Mother was an alcoholic who drifted from town to town, a one-night stand that Jonah regretted right away, then tried to work into a relationship when she sought him again, plump with his child. After the birth, she went for a long-denied drink and didn't return.

I'd always known only Jonah and Bettina, as if she'd broken off from his body entirely formed. Sometimes I watched them dance to the Spinners on the radio—*I'll be working my way back to you, babe*—and I saw how he looked at her, like she was sunshine, a natural blessing. Then Bettina waved me over, pulling my hand, making me dance even though it was awkward with three.

The three of us. We went on outings, chased squirrels in the park, strung beads on silly necklaces that Jonah made his co-workers wear, baked cookies for breakfast, and slept some hot nights outside under the stars, our girl folded like a wing between us.

Then, when Bettina was ten, well after she'd stopped sleeping between us, her mother moved back to town. Clean and sober and staying in a small apartment just across the river. She told Jonah she was in rehab and ready to retrieve the broken pieces. Bettina was so whole, a strong, healthy girl.

Jonah decided, after much fretting, that she had a right to know her mother, that short Saturday visits would be okay. Still, we couldn't enjoy those rare hours alone.

After a few months, we began to relax. Bettina had fun with her "new mom." They played old games like Mystery Date and Yahtzee and went to PG movies. They almost always ate at Bettina's favorite pizza place where once Jonah and I spied on them from the parking lot. Did two people ever look more like mother and daughter? Straight silvery-blond hair, long noses, the way their heads tipped back as they laughed.

I asked Jonah that night about us having a baby. I wanted someone who would stun me with love, who would tuck her hair behind her ear exactly like me and echo Jonah's serious words. I wanted someone to conspire with over pizza. Bettina never wanted to go there with us anymore, holding that place now as sacred. I felt, perhaps prematurely, that she was lost. Jonah stroked my hair and said, "She's our baby. She's still ours." But the next week our baby called me a bitch.

She hadn't cleaned her plate from dinner so I told her no television. We'd done this a hundred times before where she'd just sigh over her own forgetfulness then go to her room to draw or build shoebox apartments for her stuffed toys. This time she held the remote in one hand and said, "You're such a bitch."

I wasn't sure I heard right and, like a fool, stuttered, "What? What did you say?"

Now Bettina looked surprised and afraid, but she held her ground. "I said you're a bitch." Her bottom lip shook.

I wasn't angry, not even hurt yet, just shocked. "But why? Why would you think that?"

She shrugged, pulling herself into a knot in the armchair. She sobbed. I did what I always had, circled her body with my arms and pulled her in close. And I heard her through a garble of snot and tears say she didn't know why she said that and would I not tell her dad, please?

I didn't tell her dad, but later I lay awake, trying to remember if she'd said she was sorry. I wished for stars on my ceiling, the gentle fade as they surrendered their light.

Bettina came back one Saturday, wet from the rain and smelling of alcohol, something cheap and sweet. Not on her breath, but on her clothes, her skin.

Jonah leaned in at my urging and inhaled. "Bettina," he said as calmly as he could. "Why do you smell funny?"

She shrugged. "I smell like me. And I told you before. I want to be called Tina."

"Bettina," I said firmly. "You smell like liquor. Have you been drinking liquor?"

She looked horrified and furious all at once. She said that I only thought bad things about her and her mom. "I hate you!"

"Answer the question!" Jonah's voice rose in rare fury.

"Yes!" our girl shouted, adding that she got drunk all the time, "wasted, totally smashed."

We were stunned into short, hot silence. She was ten years old. She was saying "wasted" and "smashed." She was saying "I hate you" with more fervor than she'd ever said "I love you."

I watched all this register in Jonah's face, a storm eclipsing the sunshine Bettina radiated even in anger. His jaw flexed, his eyes sought to pierce through her to the truth. She'd never come home drunk, only giddy from a good time, but she'd never spoken like this before either.

Jonah snatched his jacket from the closet. "I'm going to talk to her."

"Just call, Jonah. It's late, it's raining. Or better yet, we'll talk to her next weekend."

"There won't be a next weekend if this shit keeps up."

Bettina's eyes widened a moment before tearing over. He never swore, he never threatened to take anything away from her. I saw how scared he was.

"You can't call?"

He looked at his daughter, then to me. The message registered. He didn't want her to hear his venom. "I won't be gone long. Love you both." He tried to reach out and ruffle Bettina's hair, but she pulled away and ran to her room. "Just let her be," he advised before reaching for his motorcycle helmet and dipping into the wet night.

Once, when I told Bettina that her dad and I met at a costume party, she asked in all sincerity, "Who was the bunny and who was the pirate?" She wouldn't accept that Jonah wasn't the cuddly one. Then she said, "I want to go to a dress-up party too."

"No, princess," I said. "You can't go to a costume ball."

"Why not?"

"Because we don't want you to ever be anyone but your own sweet self." Then I tickled her to hear her shrieks.

◆   ◆   ◆

Jonah wasn't back before I put Bettina to bed. By the time I tucked the sheets up to her chin and pressed a kiss to her forehead, she was our girl once more, asking timidly, "Will I be able to see my mom again?"

"Of course," I chirped. "We'll work it out."

"It was only vanilla."

"What do you mean?"

"Vanilla from my mom's cupboard. I put it on as perfume. I didn't think it would smell so bad." She sniffled, new tears streaming down her pink cheeks, and I had to smile.

"Vanilla? You should have told us." I winced to imagine Jonah's accusations.

"I know." She sniffled. "Your vanilla lotion always smells so good."

I hugged her close so she could catch the last traces of it. "It's perfumed," I said. "It's not the same as the stuff that goes in cakes."

"I know that now." She blinked and I laughed, turning the dimmer so her stars could emerge.

It was well after midnight when I heard someone on the porch. I turned on the light, opened the door, and felt my blood sink to my feet to see two police officers. I wanted to believe he'd hit her and was hunched in a concrete cell, head in his hands. But that wasn't Jonah and never could be.

It was a scene from a movie, my swoon and collapse. No more expected than the careless turn on a wet street, the truck whose worthless brakes would squeal through me many nights. One of the officers helped me to the couch, the other asked if there was anyone he should call. I couldn't think of anyone I'd want. Except Jonah.

After the officers left, I went in to look at her. I leaned in close and her heat radiated up. And then it was too much, this breath hot and alive, so I went to the porch where the sky was a flat silver mist and cold. Unbelievably cold.

◆　　◆　　◆

At the funeral, I saw how people looked at us, me and Bettina wearing our costumes of plain black dresses and stunned white faces. I saw the pity like a tidal wave always just hovering over our heads, the silent questions—*Who would take care of the little girl? Where is her mother?* And the questions offended me. I would. She was our girl.

We ate sympathy casseroles until our stomachs cramped, we wept in each other's arms, but we rarely spoke. Words felt ridiculous in my mouth, pieces of fluff. Then, only one week after miming our way through pain, Bettina asked, "Am I going to my mother's today?"

The sun bled through our curtains, beaming a line of light between us on the table. My fingers crept inevitably to the light, then my hand. The beam glanced off my ring onto a wall, splattering a radiant stain. I wanted to scream, *Are you fucking insane?* But she was ten. And I was still sick with the impotence of words. I said, "No."

"Next week?" She leaned forward on the table, her eyes bright with tears. The way she crouched there looked so much like Jonah when he worried over money. Strange how she mimicked her mother's laugh but her father's anxiety. I wondered if she took anything from me or if genetics always triumphed.

"I don't know, Bettina."

"Tina."

"I just don't know."

I heard her on the phone later, low urgent whispers and sobs she couldn't stifle. *No, Cinderella, you can't go to the ball.*

The next week we returned—she to school and me to work, and I had to leave the bank twice to pick her up because she couldn't stop crying in class. The first time I took her for a Dairy Queen sundae and she threw up hot fudge all over the car. The second time I took her home to bed and gave her ice cubes to nibble and press to her puffy eyes. I went to the living room, curled up on the couch where we all once sat together, and sucked on a cube myself.

I decided then, hearing the horrible cries, that I not only hated words but all human sounds. I wanted to live in a world of perfect silence. Like Jonah. At the bank, my manager moved me upstairs to sort checks in a blank cubicle. I could hear only the hum of the air-conditioning system. I was grateful and so were my co-workers. Before I appeared, I could hear them joking. Sometimes I'd stand, hidden in the stairwell or around a corner, and listen to the music of their laughter.

On Saturday, two weeks after I lost him, I sorted his clothes for the Goodwill. My sister, who'd never met Jonah, said I should, that too many people clung to the things themselves. Pulling out his dress shirts, I understood why. They smelled like him, as though any minute he'd walk in from the shower and pluck it from my hand with a "hey, thanks" and a smile. Instead, Bettina came through the door, picking up a corduroy jacket I'd never seen him wear, then putting it on backwards like an art smock or a straitjacket. She posed in the mirror. She put it on right, and then she began to cry.

"I want him to come back," she said, her shoulders shaking so the jacket seemed to dance.

"Me too."

"Show me his pirate outfit, what he wore to meet you."

"I can't," I said. "It was a rental."

"Then show me something he had with him that first day," she insisted, spinning around the room to pluck things from the dresser. Her tears were storms starting and ending with alarming speed. "What about this?"

"Your dad's pocket watch. It was his dad's."

"Did he have it when he met you?"

"I don't remember," I said, my fingers fluttering helplessly.

At the party, he'd pulled the tarnished watch from his trousers at ten minutes to midnight, snapping it open with a self-confident, sexy flair. He said he was sorry, but he had to leave.

"Does somebody turn into a pumpkin?" I asked, trying to be cute, though I was certain I'd somehow lost his attention, not once expecting a babysitter's curfew.

"Somebody might," he replied, adding, "But if you're leaving, I could give you a lift."

"I have no reason to stay."

He lifted me onto the back of his bike, Captain Hook and his half-drunk bunny trying to beat the clock.

Bettina dropped the watch in the pocket of that corduroy jacket. She moved on to study our wedding picture as if she hadn't seen it every day for three years. "You didn't have this the day you met," she said, pressing her thumb over her own face. In the photo, her nose was tipped down to the bouquet of lilies and forget-me-nots clutched in my hand.

I simply nodded and watched her finger the evidence that I'd loved someone and he'd loved me back. Sitting in a pile of clothes thrown about like rags but smelling of him, I watched. I wound a tie around my wrist to keep from snatching the cotton rabbit tail from her hands.

"Is this a powder puff for makeup?" she asked, patting her nose.

"Yes."

"Not my dad's then." She tossed it back on the dresser and it slid off and behind.

Bettina began draping my necklaces over her head, somber as someone awarding medals. In that jacket and my jewels, she looked half pimp/half old-maid scholar. Eyeing herself in the mirror, she said, "I've got a little of both of you now, don't I?" I couldn't answer that or the girlish sobs that soon gurgled up.

The Real Mother called later that day. She said, without identifying herself, "I'll pick up Tina around five?"

"There's no one here by that name," I said automatically.

"Okay, then. I'll pick up *Bettina*."

I had no idea who I was speaking to, I'd never heard the voice before, and I wondered for a wild, desperate moment if she was being taken away to foster care and no one had told me. When the caller mentioned Paolo's Pizza, I knew.

"You're her mother."

"Of course." She said it like that. Of course. Like it was obvious. Like she hadn't been MIA for ninety percent of her child's life.

I held the phone close to my mouth and whispered, "You know about Jonah?"

She was quiet, then she said that yes, she knew and she was so sorry, especially for her daughter. She said she hadn't called last week out of respect.

"But now that it's been two weeks, you have no more respect?" I instantly regretted the sarcasm.

"Of course not." She choked up, then continued. "But don't you think it's important that we keep things how they were before? Routine is so helpful in a crisis."

"How they were before. Sounds like a fairy tale to me. Make-believe."

A long pause on the other end. I thought she might have set the phone down to use the toilet or get a drink. But she said softly, "Okay." Then, "Can I take Tina for pizza?"

I'd grown so tired of my own voice that I merely nodded.

"Hello?" she echoed into the phone. "Hell-o?"

"Fine," I said. Then she hung up and the awful sound of nothing filled my ear.

We picked up where we'd left off then, and I never asked the Real Mother whether Jonah had made it to her apartment that night or not. How quickly was I notified? Which direction was his motorcycle headed, toward or away? Did he ever learn that his daughter had only splashed herself with vanilla, that she was still our little girl and not a preteen alcoholic? These were questions I didn't really want answered, so I let Bettina bound out to the waiting car and sat alone in the dark, imagining mother and daughter laughing, maybe crying and holding each other in some impossibly perfect bond.

I hoped, as the minutes lurched into hours, that she would really come home, then felt a spasm of surprise when she did, right on time. She slammed the door behind her, looking wildly around until she saw me curled on the sofa. And we both stared a moment, as though the other were an intruder, before I asked if she had fun and she said yes.

Then it came, what I'd feared and expected all along. One day Bettina said she wanted to move in with her mother. She sat at the kitchen table playing with her mashed potatoes, afraid to meet my eyes as she softly argued, "She *is* my *mother*."

I said, "No. Your father would have wanted you here."

"He's not here." She still wouldn't look at me, but tears trembled over her lower lashes. Her potatoes swirled into a shallow bed, an empty lake.

"I'm here," I said, wishing my voice didn't sound so far away. "It's best that we're together."

Bettina pushed her spoon down so fast that potato spattered across the table, white grainy blobs I would forget to wipe up before they hardened like scabs. "I'm going and you can't stop me!" she screamed, running to her room while I sat there dazed, seemingly remembering those words from a long, long time ago.

She was right. I could do nothing, not when her wishes were so clear to the judge. "I want to live with my mom." And she wept, clinging to the pale blond woman who'd birthed her. The Real Mother looked in a panic, unsure what to do. Her hand patted Bettina's back while her eyes searched the titles of the judge's leather books like they secreted spells that could be used against her.

Later the judge said she was sorry. "Why didn't you legally adopt her? There would have been no question."

But Jonah had said she was ours.

Bettina sobbed in my arms when her mother came to get her. How many tears could one child hold? She'd shed enough for us both. She'd dry up. Her suitcase and four boxes of toys and mementos, including Jonah's pocket watch, waited by the door. She promised she'd call as much as she could. She said she loved me and I could tell she meant it.

After they drove away, I saw where she'd pressed her face to my silk blouse—a wet bloom ruining the fabric. I tucked it in the back of my closet with Jonah's clothes.

Bettina kept her promise to call and I took her for ice cream a few times, sneaking in questions about her mother, looking for any thread I could pull to unravel them and bring her back. I spent long nights on the porch, watching the real stars prick through the night, wondering how hard I'd tried before.

"I bought a puppy," I told her on one of those outings, half-hoping she'd want to come home with me where I'd lock the doors and never let her leave.

"Really? Mom got me a kitten. She's black and her name's Kim."

I thought of the freckled spaniel locked in the bathroom, nameless, peeing on newspaper, howling with loneliness. I said, "So we both have pets."

"Yeah," she said. "Maybe they should meet and be friends."

"Maybe. Your dad never liked dogs. He thought they were too much work."

"He loved dogs!"

"No, he didn't. He said they were whiny and needy."

An elderly gentleman in suspenders interrupted us. He leaned down, smiling sweetly, and said, "Your daughter's a pretty young lady." Bettina blushed and said her gracious thanks, but I only stared at him, strangely resentful.

"I've got to get home," I said when the man walked away.

"Why?"

"I'll turn into a pumpkin," I answered. More like a jack-o'-lantern.

The weeks between dessert dates stretched and stretched. A rubber band losing all elasticity. We both knew it would snap sooner or later. Our conversations stuttered and stopped over the smallest things. Bettina would show me her green eye shadow or brag about how she could stay up past midnight. I'd say that was inappropriate for a girl her age, and she'd stare into her ice cream. A dead look, like she couldn't see me. I wished she'd splatter her ice cream all over me. This time I wouldn't let her run away. I would stop her and hold her and insist on happily every after. I'd make her listen to those old stories again and again.

She stopped having time for ice cream. Always other plans, nothing she'd specify. And though over the next few years I got annual Christmas cards signed from her and her mother, she stopped returning my calls. Sometimes I slept in her old room to pick out constellations in the jumble of invented stars on her ceiling. The one that looked like a cross I called Burden Major, and its companion, a round grouping like the Pleiades' puckered mouth, I called Burden Minor. Then I changed their names. The one that looked like a hook I called Jonah, only I couldn't sleep then. I kept turning on the light, recharging the stars, scared now of the way they faded.

I wished on each and every star. I tried to imagine how she'd changed, whether she looked more like Jonah with each passing year. The dog, who I'd long ago named Happy, snored at my side, his hot breath stirring the hairs on my arm.

One afternoon after work, I took Happy for a walk in the city's largest park. I had a crush on Robert, the groundskeeper who always stopped pruning the shrubs to scratch Happy's belly and ask me about my day. Every time, I told him how management, a position I'd obsessively and unwittingly worked myself into, was too much responsibility. Every time, he answered that I seemed like someone who managed well. He meant it as a compliment.

That day I launched into a story of the new teller, a perky young elementary ed major who counted out money in a singsong voice. I imitated her, "And that'll be FIVE, ten,

FIFteen, TWENTY!" Then I saw our girl. I recognized her sunny hair, frizzier, and that lithe young body stretched now to my own height.

"Bettina!" I shouted. She didn't turn around. She was smoking a cigarette, talking lazily to a tattooed boy with gnarled hair and something sparkling from his lip which turned out to be a diamond stud.

"Bettina?" Happy whined at the urgency in my voice and wet the sidewalk, his usual, frustrating response to stress.

The groundskeeper sensed something brewing and played with the dog. He rubbed Happy's ears and whispered, "Atta boy."

She turned around then, her face cross until she saw me. "Jamie?" She grinned and looked for a moment so much like the seven-year-old I'd first met that I held my arms out for her to bound into. She walked over slowly, the wary boy trailing, his lip stud winking like a bead of drool.

"I was wondering who'd call me by that goofy name. I beat up the last girl who did." She smiled, but I couldn't tell if she was kidding. She turned her head and exhaled a dirty cloud of smoke.

"You look—" I searched for the word, looking to Robert and the dog for help. Because I wanted to say *horrible.* She hadn't bathed in a while, her clothes were shabby and too tight, her eyes bloodshot like she'd been cursed to cry from the day she left. "You look grown-up."

Bettina laughed. "I can't even vote yet."

"Not that you'd want to," growled the boy beside her. He had small, close eyes and big teeth, stained yellow from nicotine.

"This is Todd," she said, waving her cigarette his way. Her free hand swept restlessly over her bare arm. "Todd, this is Jamie. She used to be my…she was married to Jonah when he died."

Robert kept rubbing Happy's head, but he sneaked a look at me. I could feel it.

"Yo," said Todd. *Pick a real prince,* I wanted to cry. I knew now how the wolves disguised themselves as princes, the princes as villains with dangerous hooks.

"So how have you been?" I asked, urgent when I saw her eyes wandering through the park like she'd soon follow. Those thin fingers strummed the side of her jeans.

"Surviving."

"How's your cat?"

Bettina looked at me like I was crazy, then something flickered in her face. "Oh, that black cat? It ran away a couple of years ago. Is this your dog?"

I nodded dumbly, aware of how idiotic the conversation had become.

"His name's Happy," Robert volunteered, his fingers still rolling around the drooling dog's ears. Bettina and her boyfriend exchanged smug smiles and I wanted to shout that I had named him with a heart full of irony. But I tried one more time.

"How's school going for you?"

Now Bettina and the boyfriend laughed aloud, and she lit another cigarette, saying after her first drag, "The best it's ever been. They let you stop going when you're sixteen."

"Who let you stop?"

"Anyone. Everyone," she said loudly, adding, "I can do whatever I want." She smoked faster then, nervous puffs. She flicked her butt to smolder on the grass. She strummed her fingers along the inside of her wrist then asked me for the time. "We have somewhere to be."

"What happened to your pocket watch?"

She met my eyes, held them a long moment, and shrugged. "I'm not sure. Me and Todd really have to go now."

"It was good seeing you," I said, meaning it, hoping my voice would reliably convey that.

"Likewise," she said, starting to walk away, then turning to give me a fast hug. She smelled like fruit left too long in the sun, sweet rot's beginning, and her fingers clutched me so hard I expected dime-sized bruises.

"Bettina?" I called, but she just waved over her shoulder and she and the boyfriend shuffled across the grass, receding.

Robert and I watched them go, and he finally asked, "Relative of yours?" He tweezed the cigarette butt from the grass with his fingers and dropped it into a pop can in the garbage.

"No. I mean yes. Why did you think that?"

"The way her fingers wander all over like they're searching for something to hang onto. It's something you do." He smiled shyly.

I looked down at my own fingers winding and unwinding Happy's leash. I handed the leash to Robert and held out my hands, palms turned out like a traffic officer blindly expecting all trucks to obey.

Stop, they commanded. Just stop.

CAST AGAIN

I could have picked any time in our journey before that steep mountain road to blurt my question, but my courage crested there as I peeked over the edge to where cabins dotted the valley meadow like Monopoly hotels. I hoped Will would forgive me and that he'd stay on the road as we descended.

"So when do you think we can start a family?"

He swallowed his Skoal, his throat convulsing. But he kept his eyes on the winding road, guiding the truck in its lowest gear along the gravel, hugging the cliffside. A branch batted his window, but I was the one who flinched.

"I don't know." His voice was flat as shale, but I pressed on with my mission, amused by my insistence, thinking it evidence enough that I could be a mother.

"Do you *want* a family?" I watched as a chipmunk bounded away from our tires and under a bush. I realized I was holding my breath.

"Darla," he said. "I have a family."

"You mean Kenny and Rob." They were his boys, aged sixteen and fourteen, two tall Nordic creatures who must have favored their mother's side of the family. Will was short and darker, looking more like a servant to those young princes than their father.

"And you. You're family."

"We're not married," I reminded him. "If you swerved off this mountain right now I wouldn't even get the money to bury you."

"Darla," he said, suppressing a grin. "You'd go with me."

I looked down at the dense forest of ponderosa pine, glimpses of the river weaving through the sunny valley like a silver thread. I imagined the truck rolling, the flames bursting, our two bodies charred together in a wilderness we'd come to love. I almost closed my eyes and said, "Okay." But there was no one to inherit those tangible pieces of the world that mattered to me—my collection of pressed wildflowers—forty-two kinds—the wedding china my dead mother had left me, stored still in its white padded suitcases. The boys would find them in our apartment and throw them out, shaking their blond heads or, worse, smash the dishes because they had no patience for fragile things.

I was thinking of how to bring the conversation back to that baby just starting to evolve in my mind when another truck appeared around the bend, engine whining.

"Ah shit," Will said, looking over his shoulder to back up. The narrow mountain road was cut for one vehicle and one vehicle only, and the guy working against gravity had the right of way. Will ground the truck into reverse, retracing his route up to the switchback where he could park on the side.

When the driver passed, he raised the friendly pointer finger in thanks, and Will responded in like, saying afterwards, "Don't know who the hell that is. Gets to where the whole canyon is changing. Nobody hangs onto anything anymore."

Will had owned the cabin in the canyon for twenty years. It was the only thing he'd asked for in the divorce and the only thing he got. It was the reason we lived in a two-bedroom apartment on the edge of a dying town, but I didn't mind. In the six years we'd been together, we'd vacationed only at the cabin, and I loved it as much as he did. I fished and took long walks alone by the river, especially those weekends when the boys were along. Sometimes I'd sneak a tube from a nearby cabin and float the lazy stretches of the river, browning my skin. When winter snows came and shut the road for the season, we both moped, watched too much TV, and added to our layers of fat while the hibernating bears consumed theirs.

It was early in the season, river still high and full of rafters, grass still green from the runoff. By August, the water would recede and you could walk out on the dull rocks and watch the fish pretending to hide in the holes. The rafters would be gone though, and then you'd feel you really had the place to yourself. You and the bears and the mountain lions and the countless, nameless birds flitting between trees.

Will unlocked the pump, and I lit the ancient propane fridge to cool our beers and steaks. I took the dust cover off the bed, opened the windows, then went out on the porch to sit and think.

Of course I thought of the baby, minnow splishing in my mind's recesses. My best friend from high school, Bonnie, had been knocked up at sixteen, and she had a son Kenny's age. When I hooked up with Will, she'd been delighted. "Finally," she said, "someone I know who understands adolescent boys."

But I didn't. I wasn't sure they even knew I existed except that the lemon bars I made when they stayed over disappeared within hours. I considered that a compliment and a challenge, so each weekend I made more and more treats—Rice Krispies treats, apple cobbler, butterscotch squares, peanut butter cookies with those crisscross fork patterns—and still they left only crumbs. They were insatiable, and to tell the truth, it scared me. The boys grew older and larger, and they kept eating. When I told Will I thought they might devour us, he rolled his eyes like I'd said I'd seen Bigfoot. He said, "Darla, Darla." And I knew that meant I was being silly again.

As I sat on the porch staring up at the red cliffs, I tried to think of the baby I'd have, but it wasn't there. It had slid into some deep crevice in my brain, waiting to be coaxed out by both its future parents. I'd never imagined that Will wouldn't want another child, and for a moment I felt that comfortable groove, self-pity, my butt sliding right for it, ready to park and stay awhile. Then I saw a new baby in my mind, one who looked nothing like me and only a little like Will with its black hair.

It was a Chinese baby. A girl. I'd heard how they were limited on kids over there and they all wanted boys so the girls were thrown out or smothered or sold to Thai sex traders. They were out there, all those Chinese girls, waiting.

I knew then that one of them was calling to me. Maybe she wasn't even born yet. Maybe her mother was just beginning to vomit, hoping this time it would have a penis and her husband's name to carry through the ages. But she was a girl, fragile with hope, telling me already that I didn't need Will or even viable eggs. She would be my baby, a girl, dark of skin, darker of hair, hard-wired for a language Will's boys could never get their thick tongues around.

I closed my eyes and let the sweeping wind tangle my hair. I began to dream names for her, my Chinese baby. I knew no Chinese and only two words in Japanese. *Sayonara* and *sushi*. What mother would name a girl either of those? So I dared to dream American names to call my own little girl. She would have to speak English anyway.

By the time Will set foot on the porch, I'd settled on Angela Grace, a name that fit the kind of child who'd speak from a womb halfway across the globe. "What? Are you mad at me for something?" he grumbled.

I opened one eye, squinting at the long, dark shadow he made. "No, I'm just thinking."

"About what?" Suspicious, his tongue feeling for a "Darla, Darla" to stop me in my tracks.

"Names for the baby girl I'm going to adopt from China."

He shook his head, packed fresh tobacco in his cheek. He didn't have to say anything. But he did.

"Why the hell would you want a Chinese baby? They're all damn Communists."

"Not if you raise them right. They can be Americans."

Now he laughed. "Chinese can be American. Just listen to yourself. Let's go fishing."

I listened to the bird calls for a moment. Catbirds sounding like lost baby kittens, they called to me too.

"We could get a kitten instead," I offered, but I knew he was allergic.

Will walked inside to check his lures and grab his waders. It was the wrong time of day, hot afternoon, but I went in for my rod, thinking it would feel good just to cast again and again.

"We could always have our own. Hundred-percent American," I reminded him while sorting through a tray of colorful lures, my courage evaporating fast.

Will kept fiddling with his fly rod and finally answered, "Yes, Darla, I think passing along your mother's genes is a brilliant idea."

I pinched my leg to stay the tears. Diagnosed a schizophrenic when I was only ten, she'd died by her own hand long before I met Will. I'd been raised by neighbors who parceled out her possessions to me, photos and recipes and trinkets instead of visits to see her during her long stays in the state hospital. The wedding china was for my eighteenth birthday, when they decided it was time for me to move on.

Once Will joked that I'd inherited my mother's craziness. But he only did that once.

We walked in silence down to the river, Will in front, boots squashing and squeaking through the tall grass, me five feet behind. We passed wild raspberry and huckleberry bushes, still a month from bearing fruit. Everything seemed so far from ripening that day.

Of course I went back to my baby girl. She was born by the time we reached the river, so pink and yellow and blood-streaked you couldn't tell what nationality she was. Her first cry for air sounded like my name. And I heard her father, disappointed again, moaning in Mandarin that all girls were good for was cooking and cleaning.

Sometimes cooking and cleaning was all I felt good for. I was exhausted after Will's boys visited. Only every other weekend, but they went through all the dishes (except my mother's wedding china, packed away, dustless, the legacy I'd leave, lasting as the bone that gave the china its name), and they muddied their clothes and spilled soda pop on the rug. I swear Will didn't even notice. When their mother's silver Saab pulled to the curb on Sunday, they hugged their dad, waved to me, and vanished, leaving themselves behind in a hundred ways. Bright-blue gel toothpaste in the sinks, chocolate chips smeared into the couch, sometimes a pair of dirty underwear hanging on a lamp like a soiled flag of surrender. But I knew they'd never give up. They'd just keep eating and encroaching until my camp was theirs, the battle lost before I decided to fight.

Angela Grace was a noisy girl too. She was everywhere, her wails filling the apartment like water churning in a storm. But she was my noise, my announcement of belonging, my bright claim flag, and I didn't mind. I went with it, bobbing in her surf.

"Do you want to walk down to Big Rock?" Will glanced at my flip-flops, sure I wouldn't make it through all the crossings, not with the fast current and those slick rocks.

I shrugged, imagining myself dreamy and easy while Angela, who would never be an Angie, sucked at my breast. I knew this was pure fantasy, that I couldn't give milk to an adopted baby, but I felt it just the same, the hot needle of milk stitching my breast.

"Are you okay?" Will dropped his favorite fly rod and rushed to my side. I was clutching at my chest, and I didn't even know it. I felt hot tears, real tears, splash on my arms.

"Bug bite," I gasped, blinking the tears away.

"You're sure you're okay?" Will stared at me like a new specimen of fly, a hatchling he'd study to imitate on a wet fly. Fool the fish in their foam pools. Catch a big brown.

"I'm okay." I smiled and forged on, into the first part of the river where the water rocked me suddenly, threatening to sweep me downstream. "Sorry, baby girl," I whispered. My mind had to be with the water, and I studied the current, stepped carefully, and made it across to the weedy field to wait for Will.

"We can rest for a few minutes," he said when he clomped up the shore. He watched as a large yellow raft swept over where we'd been. The young men wedged in with their camping gear gave short waves, intent on fishing the holes as they bobbed along.

"No, let's keep going."

He nodded, and I knew I'd answered exactly how he wanted me to, but then as we got into our walking trance and I brushed through thistles, I searched for Angela. I couldn't find her. Had she been lost in the stream, slipping away while my mind was on my own survival? What kind of mother was I?

I tried not to panic as I walked through a cloud of newly hatched trico. They caught in my hair, clung to my T-shirt, and one flew right in my eye, sticking in the pink corner where I could feel it wiggling. It takes more guts to feel the taut muscles of a struggling trout seeking the stream as you wriggle the hook from its lip, but on this afternoon the stuck fly rattled me.

With a shaky finger I wiped it out, stopping to stare at the black curl of its body, the wings gone gummy from my eye. I wiped it on my pants and hurried after Will, calling all the time in my mind for Angela. Angela Grace.

She had large, bright eyes, burnt almonds in her smooth face. And I saw her black curtain of bangs, almost like Will's, only straighter, and the dimples in her pudgy arms. She was a little girl, not a baby anymore, and I thought *no, no, you can't get any larger.* I saw her begin to devour the spaces around me, the very air I wanted to breathe. *No.*

"Let's stop and fish here," I suggested, and though Will didn't look pleased, he quickly set his cast and began to search for the big ones, his wrist sure in its every flick, stopping whenever he saw rafters, not so much for them, but so they wouldn't see where he was aiming.

I first met Will at the Boot Scoot. He was one of a dozen men stooped at the bar, a watery beer before him, and I was with Bonnie, who'd got her mother to babysit that weekend. Will was the only one to send over a drink, and he waited until I thanked him to say he liked how I sang along to the jukebox as if no one else were there. I know I blushed, remembering the Tammy Wynette song to which I'd given my all, but he said, "No, I like it. I like that you're a little kooky."

And of course they say that what attracts you to someone is what drives you crazy eventually. *Darla, Darla*, he said, every year the teasing tone ebbing away.

At first I loved how attached he was to his boys. He showed me their pictures the first night we had dinner. His eyes were teary, or maybe the candlelight was shimmering just right. His eyes are dark green, like the holes where the big trout hang still as ornaments in the water. I'm always searching those eyes, wondering what lures could possibly work. I still don't know how I landed him in the first place. I made lemon bars for his boys. I washed more clothes than I had in my own closet. Is that all it takes? Would my Chinese baby stay if I gave her a sweet tooth and a sense of fashion?

I threw my line in the river, just over a big rock so the spinner would sweep down to where the trout waited for the snacks that washed into their open mouths. But they didn't take my bait. After ten casts without even a nibble, the rule Will and I followed, I signaled for a shift downstream.

Will held up his index finger, no longer a country greeting, but a plea. One more cast. I nodded, and he sent his line soaring right over my spot to a still pool where I could see the trout topping. I saw his line tighten, heard the whoop he's never been able to suppress at the moment of strike, and Will brought in a pan-sized rainbow.

"The problem with you, Darla," he began as he worked the hook, "is that you never change your lures." The fish dropped to the rocks, flipping up wildly a few times before Will untied his club.

He was right. Whether from laziness or stubbornness, I stuck to the same thing over and over. Sometimes it worked, sometimes it didn't. With the trico hatch, those fish weren't biting on jigs, and certainly not in the heat of the day, but I cast again anyway, sending my line into the faster water while Will picked a few more out of the pools, keeping the legals worth eating. I came up empty every time, not even a sprig of moss or slime.

"Sure you don't want to try my rod?"

"I'm sure," I said, throwing my line out again, watching a near-perfect cast ride the rapids into the holes where nothing chased my offering.

"Well, I say we head back then. I've got my limit."

I nodded, brought the line in, hooked it to the pole. "Ready." We followed the path of broken stalk weeds along the bank, and as we approached our river crossing, I heard Angela Grace, a grown girl now, say in my ear in a musical voice, "Try here. Just try it."

So she was a girl who'd grown to love this wilderness too. I should have expected as much. She would keep coming here with me after Will was dead, and she'd bring her children who would collect wildflowers and learn the names of all the birds I could never quite see.

"Will," I called. "I'm going to try here."

He shrugged and stopped, but I could see his impatience in the leg that wouldn't stop with him, kept jiggling forward as if it were sniffing out home. "Maybe I'll just clean the fish now." He searched for his filet knife while I waded out in my flip-flops until I found a good place to stand where my line could reach the rocks on the other side.

I checked the spinner, checked the line, and cast as far as I could, lobbed it so the hook hit the cliff wall and tumbled down with a quiet splash. Something struck and struck hard. I heard the whine of the line before I felt the strain.

"Jesus! Will?"

"Hang on to it!" he called, no doubt remembering the time years before when I'd dropped my pole in surprise. He bounded to my side, wiping trout blood on the sides of his waders.

I reeled and reeled, amazed at the fight in this fish. My right arm ached in its flex, and I almost asked Will to finish bringing it in. But he had the net ready, and when he scooped it, a rainbow we later measured at sixteen inches, I was almost disappointed that I'd have to throw it back. Breeding size.

"I don't know how you caught that," he said, shaking his head. "Beats all of mine."

"I wish we had a camera," I answered, watching him work the hook. The blood on his hands was smearing around the fish's mouth and gills, and I was about to tell him to wash up in the river when I realized the blood was coming from the fish, the three-pronged hook caught fast in the gills.

"Oh God," I whispered, watching those gills open and shut, trying desperately to pull in oxygen and push out the foreign object.

"Sorry, Darla," Will said a minute later, setting down the netted fish and going for his club. "We'll have to keep it after all."

I watched the fish lie still except for its flexing gills, building up its energy for a sudden flip that landed it right on the hook, forcing it deeper. More blood.

Will quieted the fish in a single, well-aimed blow, clipped the line, and put my rainbow in his pack, hook and all. "We'll do all that back at the cabin."

Another big raft, black number 103 pinned to its side, passed us slowly, swirling some in the pools. A man, a woman, a girl and a boy. All of them in sunglasses and yellow lifejackets, rods in hand.

"Any luck?" called the man to us.

"It's not luck!" Will shouted back, laughing and patting the bulge of his pack. The man gave a thumbs-up, and his whole family went back to fishing like they'd caught the scent of blood.

"It's all luck!" I yelled. Not a one of them heard me.

I don't know how I didn't get swept away crossing the river. My knees were jelly and I was exhausted, as if I'd pulled in a marlin on the open ocean instead of a medium-sized trout on a small river. And to tell the truth, I was a little angry at Angela Grace, like she'd made me hurt the fish. *You're losing it, Darla,* I told myself in the same tone Will would use. So I focused on the current and made it across to the bushes, where Will was already waiting.

When the boys were young and smaller than us both, we made them walk behind us when we went through what I call Huckleberry Alley. The bushes grew up tall and dense on either side of the footpath, and you could stumble within inches of a black bear before you knew it. I have to admit I liked those days. Not because the boys were behind, but because I was between, sandwiched into the family.

But soon they were fearless, running ahead, coaxing their dad into chasing them, and they'd turn a bend so all I could see as they raced was their rods held high, away from the thorns, like skinny fingers greeting me over the leaves as they moved away. I'd be alone in the close bushes, feeling so far behind and thinking then that it was only a temporary emotion, one that would disappear when I walked into the open meadow.

"How are you doing?" Will asked, knowing how I hate for anything to suffer.

"I'll survive," I said. He nodded, and we began the walk through Huckleberry Alley.

There shouldn't have been a bear there at that time of day when the berries were still only buds, just as I shouldn't have caught any fish on my jig during a fly hatch. But there it was, rooting, its huge black body shaking as it worked. Small, rhythmic grunts, like it was working on a factory line.

My heart stopped because the bear, so intently grubbing, hadn't seen us, and we were twenty feet away. Will put his arm back, cautioning me, then he clapped once, loud. The bear's head swiveled, and it stood suddenly, reared up with a bellow, then watched us in a silent showdown. I was slowly stepping backwards the whole time, wondering if this one had cubs, wondering if I'd fight to the death for my own children. That's when she came back to me, in the silky black hair of the bear. That was Angela, wild, become a part of everything I loved, never really mine.

"Offer it a fish," I whispered.

"Are you crazy?"

I wondered briefly if I was. What would my mother do? Feed it, dance with it? Lie down and let it claw her open? I imagined she'd walk off with it to be a bear bride in the caves where no one would think to cage her.

Will never took his eyes off the bear, just as he'd kept steady on the dangerous mountain road. The bear's nostrils started flexing, like it smelled the fish, only to me it looked like those gills, struggling for oxygen, and I screamed. Will leapt back, dropping his pack, and the bear galloped off in the other direction.

"Darla," he spat out when he could breathe. "Darla, don't ever...." That's all he could say, and we made our way cautiously through the rest of the bushes, grateful to see our cabin and no more bears.

The sun was just sliding across the cliffs when we set out the pans to clean the fish. Will was still shaky, two beers not enough to calm him. He said he'd never known me to be so loud.

"I've got it in me, I guess," is all I said, watching as he carefully slit my fish and began to scrape the insides, raspberry heart no bigger than my pinky nail. He hadn't taken out the hook, and I was fixed on that when he told me to look.

There, stitched in like sequins on either side of her, were shiny red-orange eggs, roe she would never lay made redder by the setting sun. He rotated the fish in his hands so the eggs glimmered, and I swear they looked like they were all beating, impossibly alive.

I got up and walked back to the cabin before I could see him scrape them and throw them into the trees with the rest of the useless organs. I hoped that bear would find them and treat them as a delicacy, caviar to be savored, though I'd never known a wild animal to savor anything. That, I thought, was what separated humans from animals. The ability to savor and the ability to suffer, drawing things out so long.

That night as we sat on the porch, our heads tipped to the constellations, following Ursa Major to Ursa Minor to the orienting North Star, Will cleared his throat and asked, "This Chinese baby. If you had her, what would you name her?"

For a moment I believed he'd been in my head. He can still surprise me that way. And then I was angry, having forgotten her for a while, just enjoying the night, the murmur of the river, the flutter of bats above. And now this. Again.

"What would *you* call her?" I asked. We couldn't see each other in the dark. His eyes were lost to me, and so our voices carried our messages.

He was quiet, then said, "Willow. After me. Or maybe Loretta after my mother."

I smacked a mosquito on my leg, feeling the wet smear of it. Blood, maybe my own. "I'd call her Sushi," I said. "Or maybe Sayonara."

I could feel the weight of Will thinking in the dark, and I nearly told him I was joking, but he spoke again, his voice soft as slow water.

"I like that last one. It's got a ring."

THE WIDOW'S GUIDE TO EDIBLE MUSHROOMS

Deep in the woods she hears music, not only chickadees and the percussive drill of a woodpecker, but also—she swears—the low hum of a cowboy waltz, the merest twangs like a song switched on and fizzling to sad static. Margret scans the trees, wondering if Tim has shielded himself with headphones. But he's brought instead his girlfriend. They've chosen their own, deliberate path, leaving her alone with her hallucinations. She sighs and stares up to where leaves and sunlight checker the sky, closes her eyes until she sways with dizziness. The April air is mid-60s and perfect.

The weather is the only piece of perfect in this trip she rescheduled after Tim backed out last year. He claimed he had to study for a test. And how could she argue? Tim had infuriated her and his father with his nonchalance about his future that whole first year of college. They'd threatened to stop paying if he couldn't "get his priorities straight."

This year he'd shown up at her door with a short, mean-eyed, gum-chewing girl he introduced as "My girlfriend, Rory." *What kind of name is that for a human being?* And Tim, as if reading her mind, said, "Short for Aurora." The name of the dawn, a new beginning. That kind of name.

Tim rummaged through her cabinets like he had when he'd lived there. The girl leaned against the wall, silent, squinting through heavy slashes of eyeliner, until he offered her a bar of chocolate from Margret's secret—or so she'd assumed—stash. She nodded and asked where to spit her gum. She ate in small, rapid bites like a mouse, not even glancing up when Margret mentioned it was Belgian chocolate, her favorite.

Margret shrugs off her backpack, one of those tiny parcels junior-high girls wear—black leather, big enough for a single textbook and a lip gloss. But it's a fit for Lewis, a fact she isn't sure he would have found so funny since he never asked to be cremated. She sets down the pack carefully, with reverence because this is still the love of her life, his physical essence anyway. The body that had attracted, embraced, withdrawn from, danced for, her. Now burned down as far as it can go, which is never all the way.

She bends to tighten her boot laces and finds what she's been seeking all morning. A black morel. Smoky in color, moist with an earthy aroma. She inhales deeply, trying to save this smell of spring so she can retrieve it in the frozen future.

She calls Tim, afraid to move in case she never finds the mushroom again. Turn your back and the soil seems to suck them down. So she calls out, hating the shrillness of her voice. Eventually, her stepson and his girlfriend make their way to her, following her pointer finger to the mushroom. Tim's cloth sack is flaccid and weightless over his shoulder.

"It's gorgeous," he says, and the rarity of a compliment from him, even if it's not really directed toward her, makes Margret glow. "Now I've got to find a bigger one." He laughs and walks away, scouting the ground as he goes.

"This is something we always did together every spring," Margret explains to the girl. "Lots of people hunt them, but they're tricky. See how they blend in?" She points to the morel-colored loam. "And of course Tim's dad died a little over a year ago,"—*Fifteen months, nine days*—"and we wanted to honor him by burying his ashes where we got the first good morel in his favorite hunting ground. Tim couldn't go last year, so here we are."

Margret wonders if it will be a release to let the ashes go. They've waited on a bedside table all this time, right where she sets her reading glasses before switching off the light. She is afraid of knocking the urn over. She says "good night and sleep tight" to ward against such misfortune then lies awake wondering what she would do if he spilled. Get out the Dirt Devil? Toss a pinch of him over her left shoulder?

The girl looks for Tim. Seeing he's out of earshot, she whispers, "How did he die?"

Painfully. Margret thinks of morphine shots and the low bellowing she pretended not to hear from the bed they'd set up in the family room. The sound, she thinks, of a woman in labor—only no new life waited on the other side of that pain. She thinks of the chocolate bars at home, how she failed to slip one into her jacket pocket today. How she craves the way it settles into her stomach, fills her awhile. "Stomach cancer," she says.

"Oh my God. That's awful."

Tim looks up at the tone of her voice and they exchange fluttering four-finger waves, private signals that declare they're a couple, no room for anyone else.

"Yes, awful," she echoes. Then, "Are we ready to do this, Tim?"

He will make this decision, just as he made the decision to cremate his father. Margret, in a generous impulse, had suggested it was okay to put him in the cemetery plot he'd purchased in his first year married to Tim's mother. A responsible young husband, Lewis had bought life insurance, purchased plots, set aside twenty percent of his paycheck in a savings account, always planning, even for a future as remote and far away as his own death. Then Tim was born, and—with an opposite and equal reaction to make Newton proud—the young wife and new mother had left town, taking half her clothes and their entire savings account. To Margret's suggestion, Tim said, "Absolutely not." And she was relieved.

She can still hear him saying those words, grim and determined as if trying on the mantle of what he thought an adult should be. Here he seems so tall, even stooped to survey the forest floor. Blond like his father before his father grayed, but not so easy-going. Lewis had moved on to a series of jokes as to his ex-wife's whereabouts—an unsuccessful contestant on reality TV, a shaved-head nun living out her self-imposed exile in Burma, the woman in the car in front of them who kept her blinker on to drive them all mad. Tim didn't laugh. He absorbed each idea with quiet scorn that Lewis never assumed was directed at him.

"Not quite ready. I found a few others." He gently shakes the small cloth bag he's carried since he was young. "Not as big as yours though." Of course he'll want to bury his father in the socket left by the biggest, and of course he'll want to be the one to find it. He's so intent, so single-minded on his search that he doesn't want a novice, not even his girlfriend, distracting him. Margret knows this about Tim, embraces it with pride because this competitive streak is his inheritance from her.

Margret realizes she's gone to some other zone and left the girl alone in the forest like the motherless child in a fairy tale. "Poor Tim," the girl says, shaking her head, and it seems she will say more except she's conjured him by name and suddenly he is there, roughing up her hair with his hand, demanding playfully, "Poor Tim? What am I, the crippled orphan in a Dickens novel?"

Margret blinks with surprise. She didn't know that Tim read Dickens (who did these days?). Last she knew his reading material was all magazines, *Motocross Weekly* and *Playboy*.

"Was Tiny Tim an orphan?" she wonders aloud.

The girl giggles, grabbing at the hand in her hair. "Poor Tim," she repeats, batting him playfully. "We feel bad that you couldn't find a better mushroom."

He shrugs in concession. "I've got a dozen ones half that size, but this is the king." He crouches next to the fine black morel that has waited for them. "We'll put Dad here." He scratches softly at the dirt around the tender white stalk, digging a small moat before carefully plucking it. Mud clings to the pale stalk.

Margret notes that he has his father's dropped brow when he concentrates, and she feels a momentary yearning for the past and cradles the pack instinctively to her, but after he holds up their mushroom, she offers the urn, wrapped in a flowered towel. The girl is respectfully silent, and Margret notes the wet sheen of Tim's eyes. She wants to turn away, but she unscrews the lid and slowly shakes Lewis's remains into the hole, spreading some because black morels thrive on ash like dark little phoenixes. She doesn't empty the jar, not quite. She'll keep a bit of him around for luck, her own morbid fairy dust.

Back at the house, Margret carries her pack with the nearly empty urn into her bedroom and tucks it in a corner so she can decide on a permanent location. When she returns to the kitchen, Tim is riffling through Lewis's ancient text on mushrooms, *A Guide to Friendly Fungi*. He reads aloud: "Remember: what you swallow can be a culinary delight or a catalyst for bowel disaster. Know your mushrooms."

The girl looks alarmed. "Bowel disaster?"

Margret pulls out butter and spreads silky white flour on a platter while Tim narrates a steady stream of explanation to his girlfriend.

"We usually slice them down the middle first to check for insects. Slugs, earwigs, that sort of thing." The girl's nose wrinkles. "And you can't eat them raw because most mushrooms are toxic until cooked."

"Aren't a lot of them poisonous anyway?"

"Yeah, but we wouldn't feed you those." He pets her hair briefly, and Margret turns to watch the butter to make sure it doesn't burn. It slides and bubbles like something alive. Tim runs his finger through the smooth pocket in the mushroom's cap and reads: "If you feel your insides twist and cramp, get help right away."

The girl unwraps another piece of chewing gum, and the fake minty smell momentarily overpowers the mellow aroma of browning butter. She steps back, chewing viciously, and fans herself with a piece of junk mail Margret left on the counter, an advertising circular featuring a photo of a new Jeep. "Thanks a lot, Tim," she mutters.

"You haven't even eaten any yet!"

She moans and fans herself faster. The Jeep hops up and down in front of her face like one of those street cars with hydraulics.

"You okay, babe?" Tim touches her shoulder, and again she thinks of Lewis. The coddling, the note of possession that makes her jealous. The girl sits down at the table, insisting she's all right, but Tim sits with her—children waiting for dinner to be served.

Margret isn't sure that the girl, who didn't even know Lewis, should partake in this communion, and she feels a flash of the old anger, when she'd first seen her shadowing Tim on the doorstep. That sense of intrusion. But when she serves the mushroom, she splits her half with the girl, and sets each section on small, eggshell-white plates trimmed in silver curls like flattened metal shavings. She hands out royal blue napkins, real cloth.

Tim says, "Are these plates new?"

"No, I've had them since we were married."

"I don't remember them. But I was only six." He adds this last part for the girl whose eyes have widened at the sight of the fried mushroom piece before her.

"It's wedding china. A pattern called Shooting Stars," Margret says, "and no, you wouldn't remember because we never used them." Lewis had told her it was a waste to register for things like that, but she'd insisted it was her only wedding, she wanted everything. And then it had become another joke between them, these expensive dishes stored away in padded suitcases because they didn't even own a china cabinet.

"To Dad," Tim says.

"To Lew," Margret offers quietly.

The girl just smiles, and when Margret bites in with delight—salty, full, earthy—she hasn't tasted in two years, she sees that the girl sits with her hands folded in her lap, carefully chewing her gum and staring out the kitchen window. Her eyes don't seem mean at all to Margret anymore—maybe it was only the thickness of her eyeliner—but shadowed, like she too has secret, unplumbed depths she falls into sometimes.

Tim is savoring his half of the mushroom and not paying her the same attention as before, so Margret asks, "Honey, is there something wrong with your mushroom?" She winces at that practiced saleslady endearment. *Can I help you, honey?*

"I don't really want it."

"Oh." She doesn't trust herself to say anything more. First this girl shows up uninvited (no, invited by Tim) then, when offered a delicacy—one meant to honor the life and death of her boyfriend's father—she refuses. Margret chews the last of her mushroom piece deliberately, sinking into the taste, trying not to think. She watches as Tim pinches the girl's share of the mushroom between his fingers and pops it into his mouth with a hearty "mmmmmm."

That was *my* part, Margret thinks, realizing he's had three-fourths of Lewis's mushroom. Mine to give away, mine to take back. She remembers a call from childhood games: *No takebacks.* She'd already given it away.

Tim offers to take them all to lunch, and though Margret wishes it were just the two of them sharing fond memories of Lewis, she's too surprised by the generous gesture to do anything short of leaping for her jacket. They pack together into his truck, and when Margret asks about a third seatbelt, Tim rolls his eyes and says, "Rory's used to riding bitch."

"Excuse me?"

"It's just an expression," the girl says, though she is, herself, expressionless.

Tim drives them to a diner out of town, a place she's only ever passed on her way to more purposeful destinations. She gets her own side of the booth, and it makes her feel like their counselor or inquisitor. It's lonely, and so, on top of her omelet and sausage links, she orders a large side of hash browns with cheese—Lewis's favorite—to fill up the space beside her.

The satellite radio—quite advanced for a local greasy spoon—is tuned to classic country, and Margret hears, with a start, a lonely cowboy waltz that reminds her of what she heard in the woods. She tells them the story, and they actually don't look at her like she's crazy. Tim says, "It's déjà vu." But the girl shakes her head with a strange burst of passion.

"No," she says. "It's the opposite. Margret had the memory *before* the real event."

Margret, impressed that the girl used her name, agrees. "It's like a flash of the future."

Tim scoffs. "Memories, by definition, happen *after* the event."

The girl grows more excited. "But don't you create how you remember something in advance?"

"How?" Margret asks, genuinely interested.

"Prejudgements, all the experiences you've had that shape how you see the present and future, which of course becomes the past." The girl looks pleased with herself and even Tim nods slightly.

They continue to argue about memory, devour the food, which is surprisingly good, and talk, the loose, comfortable chatter Margret can no longer manage at work. She basks in the conversation, craves its continuing all day. She learns that the girl works part-time for a children's party organizer. *As a clown.* She considers that she must save all her facial muscles for the exaggerated frowns and smiles she must conjure on the job. Or maybe, Margret thinks, looking at the thick-rimmed eyes, she lets the makeup be her face.

She discovers that the girl can make balloon animals—she's perfected a rhinoceros—and is majoring in hospitality. "Restaurant and hotel stuff," the girl explains.

"You need a degree to serve food?" Margret studies their waitress, a plump young woman with dark spots of acne under her makeup. She can't even lay the silverware straight.

Tim narrows his eyes, in case she's criticizing, but his girlfriend nods and says, "If you want to start as a manager."

"And do you?"

"Sure."

Margret, who *is* a manager, says she needs more conviction than that. The job sucks. Managers are responsible for, well, managing. Everything. From surly employees to lagging sales and monthly reports to the little, dumb things like finding safety pins to make a shirt look svelte on a mannequin.

The girl cocks her head and says, "What do you manage anyway?" Margret notices her appetite is back, that she's practically shoveling pancakes into her small mouth.

Margret sips her coffee. It's cooled so the flavor flattens on her tongue. She says, "I'm head of a women's clothing department." She doesn't say that it's *the* women's department with a capital "W." When, she always wonders, did Woman become a euphemism for plus-sized, for fat, as if anything else meant you were girlish? Her department deals in the Xs and double-Xs and even triple Xs, which her customers ask for in the same shamed whisper one might request a pornographic movie. Only they say "three X" so the number is loud, the letter barely heard.

"Do you like that?"

Margret looks at the girl, who seems bright with interest while Tim drums his long fingers on the tabletop. "Like what?"

"Managing."

"Oh. Sure."

But she hates it. She only took the training after Lewis died because she couldn't keep up mortgage payments working sales at the jewelry counter. She'd loved the slender, winking bracelets of gold, the chunky beads and sparkling earrings. She'd truly enjoyed the brief, luxurious exchange of fastening something beautiful around another woman's neck or the power of suggesting some treasure to a nervous husband overwhelmed by the glittering display. And because she had no one else on whom to bestow the benefits of her discount, her own jewelry box grew crowded with beautiful things. Lewis said the store was *making* money off her employment, but that had only been true once, the month after he died when she'd come home everyday with some secret treasure she thought he would have loved to see on her: an amethyst ring, jade earrings, a tiger's-eye pendant burnished, warm as liquid light. She never wears any of them.

And now she works in a clothing department where her own average size is a distinct disadvantage. In her first month, when she'd worked the floor—*a good manager knows every aspect of her department*—a customer had berated her after the fifth pair of pants she'd brought hadn't fit: "What in the hell would you know about my size? Let me talk to your manager."

"But that's me," she'd said, so timidly that the customer had laughed. "Take up some space in this world," the woman had advised before leaving the useless pile of pants like shed skins.

Now Margret doesn't work the floor except during the Crazy Days sale. She handles other people's problems, and she doesn't use any of her paycheck in her own department, though every time she pulls a chocolate bar from the coffee can on the top shelf of her cabinets, she thinks that's where she's headed. Eleven pounds this year. She's a size ten on her best days.

Tim finishes his breakfast with a final dip of toast crust in egg yolk, then leans in and whispers something to the girl, who looks momentarily frightened but nods.

"I've got to go make a phone call," he announces, palming his cell phone. He pets the girl's hair, gives her a look undecipherable to Margret, and walks out of sight.

The pleasant banter folds under the awkward reminder of an alliance Margret is no part of. She wonders briefly what sort of call Tim is making, fears for a moment that he's a drug dealer, but only because it's the kind of thing parents worry about, not because Tim, who's never been a troublemaker and has plenty of money from one of his father's policies, could do such a thing.

"So what's Tim majoring in now?" Margret asks, slicing straight through the tight silence with an easy starter.

"Elementary ed."

"What?"

"You know, grade-school teaching."

"I thought he was a business major."

The girl eats another enormous bite of her ham and cheese omelet and nods. "He was. Before." Her look is sly.

"Before what?" And there's that weird silence again, that instance of power—I can let you in or I can keep you out—which Margret recognizes as her own game.

"Before the baby." She says it softly then fills her mouth with more pancake, gobbling now, no longer this morning's chocolate-nibbling mouse. Syrup winks from her bottom lip.

Margret remains calm. She turns on her sympathetic smile while the radio above her croons lost love. She wants to say the right thing, but she's got to get control. Her brain is screaming like the baby that isn't yet real to her. Screaming for something she can't identify. She imagines them dropping out of school, living with her, eating her chocolate bars everyday. She sees herself pressing the bundle to her breast, consoling the child in the middle of the night because the girl needs her rest and Tim is working third shift at the local windows factory. She's waltzing the baby around the kitchen to sad cowboy songs, to immunize him against a lifetime of sadness, and he looks more like Lewis than anyone. She thinks how she could buy the girl clothing from her department by the time she reached her eighth month. Nice clothing: velvet V-necks and summer frocks, pleated career blouses.

"We're getting married in June," the girl says quickly, interpreting Margret's silence as disapproval. "And it wasn't an accident. We know how to use birth control." She says this last part defiantly.

Margret is struck by her bravery, this quiet girl who clowns for children's birthdays, who is vocationally prepared to throw her own child lavish parties and will someday manage a hotel or restaurant, making sure that strangers feel welcome.

"You planned this?"

"I know what you're thinking," the girl says, "that we're young and foolish and ought to wait until we've got stable careers."

"You don't know what I'm thinking."

"You don't think that?"

"I only said you don't know what I'm thinking."

"Oh." The girl fiddles with her empty fork, glances out the window, holds up one finger. Margret turns to glimpse Tim's back as he returns to the truck.

The girl answers her unasked question. "He wanted me to break the news."

"Why? You can have those hash browns if you want."

She nods, pulls the plate to her, pauses to choose her words. "He doesn't think you really listen to him." She carves out a chunk of the potatoes, rolls them in her mouth before swallowing.

The waitress chooses that moment to refill their water glasses—finally—and asks if they need anything else.

"Just the check," Margret says, knowing she'll pay. When the waitress saunters away, she defends herself. "Maybe *he* doesn't really talk to me." Case in point. But it's an old issue, one she debated with Lewis many times. "You're both stubborn," he concluded to her perpetual dissatisfaction.

The girl says, "He's a guy. They aren't into talking." Margret thinks how Lewis loved to talk, even when he wasn't saying anything. He filled up the room with his musical voice.

"What do your parents think about this?"

"We haven't told them. That's next."

"Your friends? What do they say?"

"We haven't told them either. You're the first."

Margret realizes the girl really has been rehearsing. For her. She should accept this gift as is, but she can't resist. "Why me?"

The girl shrugs and glances out the window again, nods almost imperceptibly, but Margret doesn't turn to look. She knows Tim is standing there, a coward waiting for the all clear. "He thought you should be the first to know. And we both figured you'd be better at maternal advice than my mom." Her laugh is bitter.

"What do I know about children? I never had any." She sees Tim strolling back to the table and recognizes the lie of his cocky walk. It is a revelation.

"You had him."

When Tim sits down, Margret says, "Are you really ready to deal with kids?" Before his face can register the insult he assumes, she adds, "Rory told me you're going to be an elementary teacher."

"I like the fourth-graders. I sat in on a class recently."

"I can picture it," Margret says. She can't. She can barely remember what Tim looked like as a fourth-grader. They get up to leave, and Margret pays the bill without a word of protest from her stepson and his, say it, soon-to-be wife.

Tim is shy with her the whole way home, formal. He asks repeatedly if she's comfortable, as if she's the one who's pregnant. Margret had insisted that Rory take the other seatbelt. "There'll be no more riding bitch," she said firmly, like a mother, before taking that place herself, legs straddling the gear shift so the sides of her widening thighs touch both of them at the same time.

At the house again they linger as if waiting for something. Margret offers water (not thirsty) then her thanks for their driving her (no problem). And still Tim and his girlfriend hang around. It's not that she doesn't want them to stay, but their earlier easy conversation has dissolved, and she's exhausted and unable to stop thinking about that chocolate. "Wait," she finally says to Rory, as if she were going somewhere, "I've got something for you." She slips into her bedroom and opens her jewelry chest, eying the never-worn baubles greedily, not sure she can do it. "Which one, Lewis?" No response from the vase in the bag in the corner of the room. Finally she chooses the tiger's-eye pendant set in gold.

When she drapes it over Rory's fragile collarbone, she says, "For luck." She's inventing that. A tiger's-eye could mean anything, anything at all, but Margret thinks it's luck they need now. Maybe, she thinks, they'll be so foolish as to pawn it. Rory fingers the stone that glows like morning. Tim, still shy as a stranger, thanks her for lunch. "I would have paid," he says.

"Someday I'll let you."

Margret watches them get in the truck. Rory is back to riding bitch, but nobody protests. Rolling down the drive in reverse, the two of them seem at the mercy of the truck itself, just along for the ride, their heads turned away to what would be the future if they weren't going backwards.

She raises her hand to give a four-fingered wave, but no one is watching. Then Rory turns, sees her, and returns the gesture.

Margret walks back into the quiet house and climbs on the counter, frantic with craving. There are still three bars, one dark chocolate, one with almonds, one plain milk chocolate. Margret pulls three of her wedding dishes from the cupboard, arranges the chocolate like elegant dinner courses, and eats them rapidly, gorging herself until she feels sick and sugar-shocked. What kind of grandmother will she be—a staunch guardian of nutrition, pusher of carrots and apples, or a shameless dinner-spoiler?

The mushroom guide is still there, a pen wedged in and buckling the pages. *The work of fungus is to break down and give back. Dead leaves, deer pellets, all are recycled into the wonders you discover each year.*

Suddenly, her body revolts against the day.

Stomach roiling, head starting a low rumbling ache, Margret enters her bedroom, intending to fold herself up, let the chocolate digest, nap if necessary. She can wake to start the day over, make coffee and toast for dinner and pretend the earth is rotating the other way as the sun sets. She glimpses the abandoned backpack, sees the jewelry box left wide open, its pirate booty shining in the afternoon sun, and the whole room feels like her stomach, too small for everything it is forced to hold.

If you feel your insides twist and cramp…

She stops and listens through the quiet, beyond the protests of digestion, to a distant gallop she recognizes as her own panicked heart. No slow, measured song, this grief. She's heard it all wrong.

Now she listens. She hears the future, sees it, sends all her senses there. This is the way she decides to remember her future: she's holding the baby closer than she's ever held anything. The kitchen window ushers in a breeze that smells like the promise of spring. They're waltzing over the kitchen floor, and the balls of her bare feet recoil from the cold so the dance is almost a tiptoe. And the baby's exhales are small, milk-scented sighs that become part of the song, become the song itself even after the young parents have arrived, a long, trembling note. Held.

THE HOUSE SETTLING

ghosts

They heard the first one as they lay beneath the sheets, her head on his shoulder. A long, slow shudder in the wall, like the house was trembling.

"Windy night," she murmured too close to his ear so the vibration of her voice hurt. Evan gently pushed her face away and sat upright.

"It was perfectly still before." He leaned forward, listening, but the strange sound had given way to the ordinary ticks of the bedroom clock and Chloe's short, shallow breaths.

"The wind," she insisted, pressing closer. He pulled back from the sticky, smothering heat of her body then tucked her in, sheets wrapped to her neck.

"Just the house settling," he said. "I'm going to check on Ryan." Evan started to slip from his side of the bed, then leaned over quickly and kissed her on the cheek. "Right back."

He stumbled in the dark hall over a box that hadn't been there before. Chloe's psychology textbooks or maybe framed photographs she meant to hang. He couldn't see the box, but he could imagine her bubble script labeling the contents and the color-coded sticker linking it to a specific room. She had so much stuff he didn't know where to store it.

His son was sleeping, thank God. Evan's first night with Chloe had nearly been the last. Ryan knocking on the door he never closed, crying over a bad dream, Chloe scrambling for a shirt, then, panicked, hiding in the closet. When Evan returned from the ritual—drink of water, flashlight check for monsters, lullaby until sleep—it was his new girlfriend who needed soothing. She said she felt foolish, she wanted to leave, but she was smiling through her tears and wearing his old T-shirt from the back of the closet that said *Where's the Beef?* He wouldn't let her go, stroked her hair until she softly snored and made Mickey Mouse pancakes in the morning.

When Evan returned from Ryan's room, he moved into her warmth and whispered, "What if it wasn't the house settling?" He wanted to frighten her, just a little, so she'd always stay close. But she was already asleep, her dark hair trapped in the corner of her mouth.

Chloe had started the coffee in her own maker. His sat to the side of the counter, cord dangling useless as a tail. "I thought we had rules about which stuff we used," he said, opening the refrigerator, then shivering as his bare chest crawled with goose bumps.

"We do," she said sweetly. "The nicest stuff. My maker's got a thermal carafe. The coffee stays warm without burning."

"What if I like burnt coffee?"

She made a pretend pout, and pulled out mugs—both his—like she'd lived there for years. Ryan came racing up from the basement where he watched cartoons, an old baby blanket tied around his shoulders. "Dad-dy! Chloe said she heard a ghost last night!"

Evan groaned. "No, she did *not*." He looked pointedly at her, but she smiled, pouring his coffee.

"I said I heard something that *might* have been a ghost. It could have been the wind, Ryan. Or squirrels in the walls."

"Do squirrels really live in walls?" He looked astonished, eager to tear holes in the plaster in search of their nests.

"No, they live in trees," Evan answered. "Remember how we see them at the park?"

The boy nodded, then looked to Chloe for confirmation. She shrugged. "One of my girlfriends had a whole family of squirrels living in her walls. Swear to God," she said, holding up her hand.

"How many?"

She shrugged again. "Too many. She had to call an exterminator."

"What's that?"

Now Chloe looked to Evan, and he looked back, blank and mute. *You started this. Don't bring me in for squirrel murder.*

She sipped her coffee then said, "It's like a landlord, the guy who tells someone it's time to move on out." She gestured on the last word and warm coffee sloshed over the mug's lip onto her hand and the floor.

Now Ryan appeared doubtful, and Evan watched his girlfriend search for paper towels. The boy said, "Chloe, squirrels do not speak English."

"You're absolutely right. The exterminator tells them to move in a language they understand. He helps them pack their bags and buys them a one-way ticket."

"To where?"

Here Chloe paused again, a smirk on her pretty mouth. Evan knew from the way her eyes cut to him that she wanted to say something smart-ass. "Are you going to help me here?"

"You're the squirrel expert."

"I mean with this mess." She indicated the brown puddle on the floor.

"Lower-left cabinet."

Ryan raised his voice. "Where do they go?"

She turned to his son and said in her exaggerated, not-quite-condescending voice, "They move to the city park of course. All those trees to choose from. It's lots better than running in walls."

Ryan seemed to consider this, and Evan reached for a paper towel.

"I would let the squirrels stay in my house," the boy said.

"No, you wouldn't," Evan said. "They'd make an awful mess. They chew wires and rip up insulation."

"I wouldn't care. Can we go to the park today?"

"I've got to unpack boxes," Chloe said. "But I bet your dad will take you."

"The Saints are playing the Rams," Evan mumbled, stooping to blot the coffee before tickling her feet with the edge of the paper towel.

"Be a Saint," she suggested.

"No, you. St. Chloe." He bowed lower and kissed her toes so she squealed.

Ryan tugged on both their shirts. "I want us all to go."

"He wants us all to go," Chloe whispered, one hand cupped lightly over each of their heads.

The park after lunch was an autumn festival—twirling leaves ablaze in the sun, decorating the still-green grass or clinging to oak branches, squirrels chasing squirrels, dogs chasing squirrels, shouting children chasing dogs and squirrels, and the fresh wind with its undertone of dry decay. Ryan ran ahead, and Evan and Chloe walked the path slowly, hand in hand.

"It's a pretty day," Chloe said, squeezing his fingers.

"The Saints are playing on this pretty day."

"And watching them lose again would only ruin it."

He laughed, conceding, and they walked quietly while Ryan turned lopsided cartwheels in the leaves, his too-long, white-gold hair glinting with every turn. Evan noticed squirrel nests snuggled high in the trees and every time he saw a branch shiver in the wind, he imagined the ghost of a squirrel running its length.

before chloe

The spring before had been Jen, an elementary-school teacher with brown eyes that widened dramatically when she spoke to children. She was an oversized Disney creature, flickering her black lashes in constant amazement, her voice going squeaky with emphatic praise. He didn't like her much, something he only admitted after she left because Evan's best friend, Mike, the one who'd introduced them, insisted she was perfect.

"She spends all day with kids," he said. "She *must* love them." And because Evan needed someone who loved him and Ryan both, he kept asking her over. He tried to let her sweet disposition stand in for love. He watched her eyes widen over everything Ryan showed her, from a truly impressive portrait of her in blue marker to a plain piece of gravel from the street. "That's EX-cellent, Ryan. WOW. So GOOD." By the end of the evening, when his son went to bed, her eyes drooped in exhaustion and she fell asleep on the couch, always missing the end of the movies they rented.

Once she said, "Maybe you could get a babysitter? We could go to a club or do something ex-CIT-ing."

But Ryan spent the whole week in daycare while Evan worked. It was enough of a drain on their financial and emotional reserves. Finally Jen widened her brown eyes and said, "I'm SOR-ry, It's not YOU. You're a-MAZ-ing. I just need something MORE." And Evan agreed, glad to be rid of the woman who only ever saw the first half of the story.

Before Jen, Debra, who was everything Evan would have wanted in a woman when he was twenty. Beautiful, sassy, sophisticated, she made his old robe sexy when she draped it around her late at night. But he was thirty, a single father, and, as he told his friend Mike, he needed someone who loved children more than push-up bras and pedicures. He let the fantasy girl go.

Lisa, the pediatric nurse, had seen everything. Burns and bruises from abuse, infections, diaper rash so bad it scarred.

She was no-nonsense compassion, a divorced woman with two kids of her own. When Evan had brought Ryan in with what turned out to be strep throat, Lisa put them both at ease, explaining what the doctor would check and why. Evan liked explanations—parenting seemed such a crapshoot otherwise, and when he returned for a follow-up and ventured a dinner invitation, she accepted. They'd talked about the signs and symptoms of juvenile diabetes, Reye's Syndrome, even the exotic but still-diagnosed scurvy. He'd added more orange juice into his son's diet, and when Ryan complained of stomach aches, Lisa discovered a less acidic brand.

They'd been great. Lisa knew kids and she knew the human body, both of which worked to Evan's advantage. Then she'd started bringing her own children over, two boys older and wilder than Ryan. He saw Ryan mutating into a monster as he emulated his new idols. Lisa thought it was cute. She spoke fondly of blended families, but he imagined these two older monsters calling him "Dad" and how he would want to discipline them but wouldn't feel it was his place, and everyone would look at him with scorn, the way he looked at parents who let their children turn into monsters.

He broke it off to save his son, and Ryan hated him briefly, for a much shorter time than he knew Lisa would.

Before these friendly glances, invitations, little tests and aching intimacies, before the long stretch of lonely despair in between, there was Ann. Wispy, flighty Ann with her white-gold hair and eyes he thought of as heartbreak blue. He rarely spoke of her.

her bed

The next time the house made its strange, shuddering noise, Chloe and Evan were in the kitchen, popping post-coital beers. Sex on the counter to be adventurous, though they both knew the distance from Ryan's room was the real advantage.

The first snow had fallen like fairy dust and as they stood at the window, arm in arm in their underwear, the sound came. Low at first, building like a train on a trestle coming closer, then nothing.

"The wind again?" Chloe asked, watching the fat flakes drift gently down. Beer droplets clung to her bottom lip, and he was tempted to wipe them off.

"Hell of a big squirrel," Evan muttered, craning his neck to see out to the street. "Maybe it was a freight truck."

"At 2 a.m.?"

They both drank from their beers, then Evan said, "Are you worried about it?"

Chloe paused. "No, not *worried*."

"Then what?" He stroked her shoulder, sure he'd never known such a perfectly rounded shoulder. Sometimes looking at her made his heart flutter and he felt, momentarily, unworthy.

"It's just that—well, that sound only happens after we make love."

Evan grinned and moved his hand to her hair, messy but still silky-soft. "Maybe the house is jealous. Maybe it's having its own orgasm."

She sipped her beer and said, "Then it comes like me. Building, building. Screeching to a stop."

He flinched at her tone, remembering the one time she'd really let go. His parents had been in town. They'd taken Ryan to see Sesame Street Live on Ice, and Evan had called her as soon as the car left the block. How she'd offered herself—shaking, clutching, crying, the floodgates so wide open. He felt blessed by her tears and all the raw need that came with it. He spontaneously asked her to move in and she'd agreed, though she'd never given him so much again, always half-listening for Ryan's stirrings.

"Anyway, I don't want to think about living in a giant vagina."

"I'd say it's more like a womb."

"Still, ew."

Evan rinsed his beer bottle, checked the locks, and guided her upstairs to sleep, but she lay beside him staring at the wall. Even as he felt his own mind methodically turning off its lights, his body surrendering to sleep, he sensed her thinking.

"What are you thinking?" he mumbled.

"That sound. I never heard it before I moved in."

"Yeah?"

"I think it's Ann."

The lights in his mind all flooded on again, and he turned to her. "What are you talking about?"

"Ryan's mom?"

"I *know* who Ann is."

Chloe paused again. "She's haunting this place. I can feel it. You said I'm the first woman to live with you since her, right?"

"Yes, but—"

"*She's* jealous, not the house. I'm fucking her husband in her kitchen, in her bedroom, maybe in her very bed." Here Chloe paused. "I'm driving her son to kindergarten and kissing him goodnight. I've unpacked all but one box, putting my things in every room of her house. She doesn't like it."

Evan didn't know what to say. He wanted to ask about the one box she hadn't unpacked, but that didn't seem to be the point. And he was stunned. Chloe hadn't seemed the superstitious type, and he'd said very little about Ann.

"First," he said, reaching for her hand in the dark. "She never lived here. I bought this house two years ago. If you're talking about haunting, your explanation makes no sense. Hell, ghosts make no sense." He thought of those branches shivering in the park, tiny squirrel ghosts dancing on them. "Secondly," and here he chose his words carefully. "Secondly, she's *gone*, Chloe. She's not coming back. But you're here." *Aren't you?*

He felt her somewhere else, like she'd slipped out of her body the way she sometimes did when they were making love.

Leaving. Not in the ecstatic slipping of self, but its opposite, where self-consciousness makes you disappear entirely. He rubbed her hip. *Stay.*

"Gone," Chloe repeated, so much weight in that single syllable that Evan saw the lie for what it was. You could call the exterminator, have him get rid of the squirrels, and still bits of their hair would remain caught in your insulation. Toothmarks in your wall. Wind-shaken branches that would always give you pause.

He sighed, thinking maybe he should come clean. He started with, "This was her bed." But he got no further because Chloe slid from the sheets, away from his reach, spending that night on her own rollaway couch, the one he'd consigned to the unfinished basement.

mike's advice

"It's better if she believes in ghosts. Seriously, dude. Do not tell her." Mike lit a cigarette and eyed a woman in tight jeans playing darts.

Evan moped over his beer, knowing he should get home soon. Chloe had a test the next day, and at such times she was less patient about entertaining Ryan.

"But what if Ann comes back?"

"Look, it's been what, four years?" Evan nodded, and Mike went on. "All that time and you've never heard from her. Not once. She's never tried to contact you or her own son, for chrissakes. Your lawyer took care of the divorce, right? That means no legal attachment, certainly no moral attachment. That crazy bitch *is* gone."

"But Chloe thinks she's dead."

"Isn't that what you've told Ryan?"

"Yes, but he doesn't even remember her. It was the only thing to do."

"I'm not here to judge."

"It's easier than saying, 'Hey, your mom didn't want us

anymore. She just left a note and a new bag of diapers and vanished.'"

Mike practiced a smoke ring, watching out of the corner of his eye to see if the dart woman could see him. "That's my point. She is *gone*. Don't go dredging her up and blowing it with Chloe. Buy a new bed then put it to good use." He grinned. "How'd you kill the bitch off anyway?"

"Huh?"

"How'd you say Ann died?"

Evan stared miserably at his empty beer glass. "An accident."

Mike laughed. "Hell, an accident is something random, beyond your control. She planned her 'death' pretty damn well."

On the drive home, Evan thought about how long it had taken him to rebuild his savings account so he could make a down payment on a house. He didn't feel anger anymore. He felt nothing, and for a moment he believed in Mike's advice. Let the not-so-dead be dead.

But Mike had also claimed that Jen was "perfect for him." *PER-fect!* And he still hung around bars picking up women in tight jeans. Evan resolved to tell Chloe the truth.

When he walked in the house, he basked in its warmth and the savory smells of baked chicken and dinner rolls. He saw Chloe's textbook on the table, but she was on the kitchen floor with Ryan, setting up an intricate maze of dominoes.

"Hi, Daddy. You don't know how cool this is." His son looked up at him, hair falling into his eyes.

"I've knocked over dominoes before."

"Not ones this cool," Ryan answered, carefully setting up a domino, measuring its distance from the one before it with his eye.

"That's the most focused I've ever seen him," Evan said, and Chloe looked up and winked. "Don't you need to study?"

"I *have* studied, *Dad*. I'm not some undergrad."

"I didn't mean anything by it, and you are an undergrad, technically."

"Technicalities aren't important," Chloe said. "I have life experience. I know how to not screw up now." She'd been a secretary for several years before returning to the local university to finish her degree, and she couldn't stand being lumped in with the lazy, undisciplined kids in her classes.

Evan heard what she said and took it as a sign. *Technicalities aren't important. I know how to not screw up.* She was so beautiful sitting cross-legged on the floor, handing dominoes to his son like each one was a gift.

"What's your test in?" He shrugged out of his coat, carefully stepping around the domino design.

"Psychology of death and dying."

He stopped cold and looked at her, but her expression hadn't changed. No sign or hidden meaning. She was content, and he wanted her to stay that way. Let her believe in ghosts.

"Ready, Daddy?"

Evan looked down at his son and his girlfriend, both of them bright-eyed with anticipation. He nodded. Ryan flicked one finger with solemn care, and they all watched as the dominoes fell, one after another, a series of stuttering clicks, strangely musical until the last one fell flat.

their bed

He had it delivered the following week. Queen-sized, cherry wood, firm mattress. The other one he had hauled away in the same truck, some second-hand donation program. As he watched the movers load it, he thought of Chloe's tears smeared on his chest. He thought of conceiving his son one drunken night before his courthouse wedding. He thought of all the remnants of his own lonely nightmares stitched into that mattress.

When Chloe returned from a study session, Ryan was already crawling over the bed, waiting to show her.

"It's new," he shouted as soon as she walked up the stairs. "For you! It's new for you!" He started to bounce to his rhyme, and Evan had to scoop him up and cover his mouth.

166   *Chauna Craig*

"What do you think?" he asked.

She looked at the bed, traced her hand over the headboard. "Nice," she said. She didn't really smile, and Evan assumed she was tired.

"You could take a nap on it now," he offered.

"No, I'll try it later."

He looked in her face for the playfulness her tone didn't offer. It wasn't there either.

"I'll take a nap on it," Ryan said.

"You don't take naps anymore."

"I know." The boy laughed, wriggled out of his father's arms, and, when he saw he wasn't the focus of their attention, scampered off to his own bedroom, singing the chorus to a mindless pop song.

"Anything wrong?" Evan ventured, hating that question because everyone, himself included, wanted only a simple no in return.

"No," she said. It wasn't what he wanted at all.

That night, he crept under the covers, spooning around her. He cradled her and pressed his face into the flowery smell of her hair. She didn't push into him or even murmur something sleepy. She stiffened, stiffened like he was a stranger.

"Chlo?"

"I'm not in the mood."

"I know. I just wondered how you liked the bed."

"The bed is fine. It was never about the bed."

"Oh." He lay there in the new bed, turning from his side to his back, deciding finally that he needed something softer. "I can exchange the mattress," he said aloud.

Chloe turned suddenly, and he saw her white, heart-shaped face luminous in the dark. "The mattress is fine. Evan, I want to bring someone in here."

"In our bed?" He was embarrassed by the shrill edge of surprise in his tone.

But Chloe laughed, her mood suddenly rising. "No, pervert. I want to bring in someone who knows ghosts."

Now Evan laughed. "You're kidding, right?"

"I'm serious. I don't think I can sleep with you again until I'm sure we're not haunted."

"Chloe, don't you think that's a little…"

"I'm serious."

He thought in silence then said, "Do whatever you have to."

"Thanks," she whispered. She slid her hand along his arm. From another room came the call: "Daddy!"

"We're definitely haunted," he muttered, reaching for his robe.

ms. extrasensory

He came home one day to find a redheaded woman in a black sweat suit pressing against his kitchen walls. She spread her fingers, placed both hands against the surface, then lay her head between, as if listening for a heartbeat. Her hips swayed a little to some music he couldn't hear.

Chloe waved at him, signaling for silence, so he went to look for his son. After searching his bedroom and the den, he returned. "Where's Ryan?"

Chloe ushered him into another room and explained in a low, secretive voice. "He's playing next door, building a snowman with the Rodgers kids. Nancy thought it would be better without his energy."

"Nancy? The psychic? Is that her?"

"Shh. She's not a psychic. She's extrasensory."

Evan tried to keep the smirk from his face. "She's fondling our house."

The woman emerged from the kitchen and said very softly, "Shall we go upstairs?" Her eyes were bright, bird-like. Her chin seemed to fade right into her neck, something Evan hated.

Chloe nodded and pointed the way. "I'll be right there."

They watched her glide up the stairs, almost floating. Evan thought she should have been wearing a flowing Indian-print skirt with those tinkly little bells dangling from the waist.

"She looks familiar," he observed.

Chloe paused and gave him a strange look. "Funny, she said the same thing about you when she saw that picture of you and Ryan at T-ball. You didn't date her, did you?"

"God, no. Too creepy."

"Must be some past-life thing then," Chloe said.

"You better get up there before she humps some spirit on our virgin bed."

"You're terrible!" But she took the stairs two at a time.

Evan returned with his pink-cheeked, sweaty son only after he saw the woman's SUV disappear down the block. A cold trickle of melted snow from a well-aimed snowball slid down his collar.

"Did Ms. Extrasensory get rid of the ghosts?" he asked, helping Ryan out of his snow suit.

"Strangers can't get rid of your ghosts," she scoffed. "Nancy only senses where they are and what they want. She detects energy. Here, have some cocoa." Two mugs waited on the table, and Ryan smiled a big thank-you, plucking his marshmallows out first.

"Well, what did she sense?"

"We can talk about that later." She said it so firmly he didn't question further. He and Ryan sat sipping their hot chocolate while Chloe gazed out the window like she was waiting for someone.

Later came and went. Still Chloe didn't speak of ghosts or Nancy. Still she slept by his side, brushing off his hand when it lingered too long at her hip.

One afternoon Ryan returned from first grade with a colored pencil drawing he wanted hung on the refrigerator. A small yellow-headed stick boy stood shadowed by a tall stick man and a shorter stick woman with black lines snaking from her round head. Above the trio hovered a stick with crude wings and long yellow hair.

"It's the anorexic nativity," Chloe announced.

"Chlo-e," whined Ryan. "It's supposed to be us. The angel's my mom."

She told him it was a nice picture and kissed him on top of the head. She pinned it square in the center of the fridge, then she put on her coat and hat and told Evan she was taking a walk.

He started the hamburgers for dinner, letting Ryan help squash the patties. They pulled out a bag of frozen French-fried potatoes as in their bachelor days.

When Chloe came back, her nose and cheeks were red with cold. Her eyes were red too. She told Ryan it was because her blood was frozen, and he snuggled up to her, rubbing her cheeks softly while she read him fairy tales.

After goodnight kisses and tuck-in time, Chloe and Evan sat in front of the TV, each waiting for the other to speak. Finally, Evan said, "Is anything wrong?"

She turned to him fiercely. "This whole house is wrong. It's haunted."

"Is that what Ms. Extrasensory told you?"

"No. She said this is a cold, closed-up, ordinary house. No spirit here. She thought maybe the sound came from the pipes."

"Then I'll have those checked. Maybe look for squirrels too." He smiled at her, thinking of christening their bed, but she didn't smile back.

"She remembered how she knew you."

"Oh?" he asked, actually curious. He remembered her vaguely, as in a dream, but couldn't figure where he would have met such a nut.

"You really don't know?"

"No."

"Nancy used to date your friend Mike."

Evan laughed. "That doesn't exactly narrow it down." But Chloe didn't laugh, and he felt his gut roll.

"Several years ago. She said she was glad you'd moved on in your life after your wife *just disappeared*."

Evan remembered how he'd been dazed with grief, how the woman Mike had been sleeping with—not dating—had claimed that if he gave her a personal object like a piece of jewelry she might be able to locate Ann. He thought even then that the woman was ridiculous. Besides, he had nothing personal of Ann's left, nothing but their child.

Evan felt haunted then. The loves he'd snuffed in this very house, snipping each one short before it could entangle him. Too sexy, too enthusiastic, too much baggage, too little. These ghosts trembled around him, shortened threads tickling his eyes as he watched Chloe's face tighten and close.

whatever's in that box

She packed boxes in the hours between classes. He saw the roll of duct tape in the junk drawer grow smaller everyday. Yet he said nothing, pretending an inevitability to be suffered in silence. He said nothing to Ryan, though he cringed when his son kissed her goodnight and said, "I love you, Chloe-Doughy."

At night when the ticking clock and her tiny breaths kept time to some sad song in his brain, he doubted she ever loved him. She only needed a cheaper place to stay while finishing her degree, she wanted the unfettered adoration of a six-year-old. Old Evan had been swindled again. But he knew in the deeper, honest, more painful places that she loved them both. Loved them really. Not gushy, theatrical emotion, not martyred duty, but simple and full and everyday love. If she left, she would do it for a reason, and she would stay in her own life, maybe bump into them at the grocery store and start to cry. But she would still buy her pasta and her gourmet coffee. She would return to her apartment and her studies, and he would know then that they'd been real, that he still was. And because he knew how she would leave, he wanted her to stay.

He came home at lunch on an unseasonably warm day to find her cramming boxes in the backseat of her car. She slid in the slush at the curb, falling once, and her jeans bloomed dark and wet up to the knee.

"What are you doing?" he asked stupidly. The snow sinking into the lawn was steaming in the sunshine, like some exotic planet that could be tropical and frozen at the same time.

She stared at him for several seconds before saying, "You know." Then she added, "I want to be out before Ryan gets home today."

"You were just going to leave him alone until I got home?"

She stared harder. "No, Evan. I wanted my things out of the house. My mom's got room, and I've made arrangements for an after-school sitter starting next week. Just who were you confusing me with?"

He shrugged as if to apologize, and she returned to the house, bringing out one last box. A sheen of sweat glinted on her forehead, the hair at her brow curling in damp wisps like large commas. As she made room for the box, he thought about that hair—wet with sweat and tears on the bed he got rid of. He'd buried his face in that mess of hair, hiding his fearful amazement, and the dark tendrils clung to his cheek.

"Wait! Chloe?" he cried, reaching his hand out though she was opening a car door a full thirty yards from his outstretched fingertips. She paused and turned her head slowly. "What was in the box?"

Her brow buckled in confusion. "What?"

"The box you never unpacked. What was in it?"

She glanced at the backseat of her car as if it were there and she could just read the label aloud. She looked back at him, teary-eyed, tired.

"There were a lot of boxes I didn't unpack. All the things that weren't as good as yours. Cheap steak knives, stuff like that. Nothing you'd want."

She got in her car, shut the door, set her hands on the steering wheel at 10 and 2, then sat immobile, eyes straight ahead like she was studying the road signs, prudently avoiding accidents.

Evan sat on the porch steps, watching her, sending telepathic messages. *Stay. Stay.*

She cranked the starter, like wrenching the key into his own gut. He sprang from the porch and sprinted down the lawn so he arrived at the driver's window with ragged breath, pink cheeks, his own jeans splattered with cold slush.

"Chloe," he gasped. "I want it. I want whatever's in that box."

She rolled down her window. "Say again?"

"I want whatever's in that box. The dullest steak knives you've got. We'll put them in the drawer. I promise."

"You're being dramatic. Do you think some movie-sounding line is going to make me forget that you don't trust me?"

"Chloe, please. I want everything. I really do. There's nothing of yours I don't want."

"Nothing? What if I have an ex-husband roaming around out there? Or a child I gave up for adoption years ago? I could be HIV positive or have a history of schizophrenia. I could believe absolutely in ghosts. I might even talk to them on a regular basis and invite them to possess me. You want all that?"

He looked at her uncertainly. He wanted to ask if any of it was true, but he realized to do so was to guide that car back into gear and press hard on the gas.

"Yes," he whispered, the warm puff of the syllable leaving his mouth as a vapor.

On their new bed, she sliced through the tape of every box they'd carried back in, pulling out an electric can opener, high-school yearbooks, towels, pencil holders—an assortment of useless and outdated things meant to be stored or given away.

"It's just junk," she laughed, self-conscious of the clutter growing around them. Then she launched into a story about how at thirteen she'd carried her dying beagle, Scraps, to the vet in this towel, how she'd gotten that Snoopy alarm clock from her mother afterwards.

"Do you think Ryan might like it?"

He nodded, and she set the clock aside, launching into a new story about the pot holders with the geese design that she hated but couldn't throw out because they'd been from the aunt she loved best. She talked, and he listened. He imagined the story he'd tell their children one day, how she sat cross-legged on their bed, her face aglow like Christmas morning, opening everything.

Acknowledgments

Thank you to Kevin Morgan Watson and Press 53 for generous support of a first-time book author. Thank you to the friends and writers who helped shape these stories: Liz Ahl, Julia Alvarez, Ron Carlson, Kate Flaherty, Sherrie Flick, Pete Fromm, Charlotte Hogg, Jean Kwok, Ladette Randolph, Jon Ritz, Rick Schweikert, the late Gerry Shapiro, Judy Slater, Marly Swick, and Sandy Yannone. For motivation, support, and advice, thank you to Tara Masih and to the Pittsburgh Intentions Group: Geeta Kothari, Jeff Oaks, Jenny Johnson, and Bill Lychack.

Thank you to these artist residencies for the invaluable gift of time and space: Vermont Studio Center, Hedgebrook, Artsmith, Virginia Center for the Creative Arts, and Ragdale. Thanks also to the original Commonplace Coffeehouse in Indiana, Pennsylvania, a refuge of good company and good coffee and the site of many hours spent editing these stories.

The people in my life who have sustained me with love, laughter, friendship, and faith are too many to name here, but these colleagues have never failed to support me in my work: Heather Powers, Krys Kaniasty, John Marsden, Mary MacLeod, Gloria Park, Lynn Botelho, Cate McClenahan, John Branscum, Michele Norwood, Sandy Greene, Yaw Asamoah, Debbie Weaver, Eric Rosenberger, and the late Wendy Carse.

Thank you to my family: my parents, Bob and Necha Craig, my brother, Kevin, my amazing cousin, Maegen, and all the Denver Connollys. Thank you to my children: without you, Andy and Ellie, many of these stories could not exist, and without you, Wyn and Zo, the person I am today would not exist. Finally, for restoring my faith in the power of genuine love and respect and for "opening everything," thank you, Dave Bright.

Chauna Craig has published stories and essays in numerous anthologies and literary journals, including *Ploughshares, Prairie Schooner, Fourth Genre,* and *Sou'wester.* She's been awarded fellowships and scholarships to Vermont Studio Center, Hedgebrook, and Bread Loaf Writers' Conference. A Montana native, she currently lives in western Pennsylvania. *The Widow's Guide to Edible Mushrooms* is her debut story collection.

Mike Davis has been a creative professional in the advertising and marketing industry for over 30 years. He spent 17 of those years as owner of his own agency before joining Nicholson Kovac in Kansas City, Missouri, as associate creative director, and as creative director at Mitchell Communications Group in Fayetteville, Arkansas. Mike earned his BS in Marketing from Park University and his MLA from Baker University. He has also taught graphic design at Maple Woods Community College. Away from the office, Mike is a professional voice talent, outdoor enthusiast, and private pilot.

CPSIA information can be obtained
at www.ICGtesting.com
Printed in the USA
BVOW06s2252110218
507867BV00001B/10/P